MYSTERIES OF WOMANHOOD

The deep undiscovered power unraveled

BY

Alison Kate

Copy wright 2022@ Alison Kate

TABLE OF CONTENTS

Introduction 3

Chapter One...17
Understanding being a lady..................................17

Chapter two...37
is child birth a plaque to women..................................37
Portrayals of birth since ages ago..................................42
Birth in Renaissance Europe..................................43

Chapter three...55
Feminisim...55
what is feminism...55

Chapter four...85
The concept of body languagein women..................................85
The study of non verbal communication..................................100

Conclusion...117

Bibliography...119

INTRODUCTION

A long time back, ladies were supposed to be spouses and moms, entrusted with raising great, moral residents and keeping agreeable homes. Most ladies didn't have vocations, except for educators, medical attendants, sewers, servants, and other people who performed positions viewed as properly female.

While there used to be a quite certain model for precisely how to be a lady — what to look like, talk, put on a good show, and plunk down and shut up like a lady — those days are a distant memory. While there are positively fights actually seething over how ladies utilize their bodies and direct their lives, the manners in which they appear on the planet are more shifted and nuanced than any other time, making the meaning of womanhood not widespread, yet rather well defined for every lady herself.

To feature the numerous ways there are to be a lady on the planet in 2020,I talked with in excess of twelve ladies to catch wind of their lives — and what being a lady implies and resembles to them. As their accounts demonstrate, being a lady isn't about privates, womanliness, or fitting one explicit shape. Every lady and her experience is interestingly hers.

'I'm an awe-inspiring phenomenon'

"Being a lady to me in my past has consistently implied being excessively. This is the very thing that I was constantly shown in my life as a youngster and puberty. At the point when somebody said I was excessively clearly or excessively chatty, it would hurt. 'A lot of' is at this point not an affront to me; it is an indication of pride. On the off chance that I am 'a lot' for the world at this time, I'm perfect for me as a lady.

"Culture has assumed an extremely fascinating part with regards to my personality and the diversity of my characters. There was a period where I never figured I could guarantee the characters of 'essayist', of 'lobbyist.' Being an Indian lady has frequently implied forfeiting one personality to safeguard another. It implied being moderate over tell the truth. To keep up with my way of life as a 'decent' Indian young lady, I needed to forfeit my way of life as a supporter for psychological wellness… Other than being a lady, I'm an essayist, a craftsman, an extremist, a trickster. I'm an awe-inspiring phenomenon, and in particular I'm 'me.' I own all of my personalities now. I endeavored to recover them all to just have one." — Vaidehi Gajjar

'Womanhood is significantly more perplexing than chromosomes'
"I think today we are seeing the earliest reference point of the acknowledgment that womanhood isn't just a bunch of body parts

and works that were never generalized to all ladies at any rate. That womanhood is considerably more perplexing than chromosomes or the capacity to convey a child.

"As a trans lady, it took me a long time to grasp that, regardless of all outward actual proof running against the norm toward the beginning of my life, my womanhood is genuine. It isn't simply an inclination nor is it fancy. It is a no nonsense, obvious power that lies profound inside me...Being a lady in 2020 isn't so delicate a thing that it can't envelop me or individuals like me.

"I'm not simply battling the man centric society and sexism for the balance of ladies, I'm battling against their belongings to be viewed as a lady by any means. That's what the net impact is, for too much, being transsexual eradicates the authenticity of my different personalities completely. Battling against that is the most women's activist thing I do." — Tune Maia Monet

'I feel associated with additional ladies — outsiders and moms and companions — than any time in recent memory'
"Being a lady implies something else to me now than it even implied a month prior. It implies I'm the supervisor of my family and I feel answerable for keeping us invigorated [on the full scale level], and furthermore assisting consistently in numerous little

ways with helping us through an emergency that is influencing the whole world.

"Being a lady in 2020, preceding the novel Covid pandemic, be that as it may, likewise has had a new, worked on importance, expanding on the two or three years since #MeToo and Folios and other female-forward drives. I feel entirely noticeable, and I feel associated with additional ladies — outsiders and moms and companions — than at any other time. It's great. It's uplifting.

"More than anything, my characters — a mother, a spouse, a little girl, a sister, an auntie, a cousin, a companion, an educator, an essayist, an entertainer, a performer — travel every which way at different times. In some cases being a sister isn't so significant similar to a mother, different times it's beginning and end at that time." — Jessica Delfino

'It implies having the decision to be strong and make some noise' "Toward the finish of 2020, I will (ideally!) be done with my most memorable semester of school at Barnard School of Columbia College. I'm an original Chinese-American 17-year-old and one of two little girls of a solitary and outsider mother.

"Like the dash in Chinese-American, I perceive how my encounters are because of the crossing point of my various characters. I was shown by my more distant family to not talk until I'm addressed and to keep silent about my viewpoint about recent developments... Being a lady in 2020 is to be proudly myself, particularly in unusual spaces that were not made for me; it means to have options in each choice I run over and to have the comprehension that every one of my encounters that have driven me to this point are credited to my different characters that converge. Being a lady to me implies having the decision to be intense and make some noise for yourself as well as passing your voice to others too." — Joyce Jiang

'I contain hoards'
"Beside being a lady, I'm undetectable crippled, a composing teacher at a school, a horrendous cerebrum injury (TBI) survivor, an independent essayist, a columnist, a heavy drinker, a rape survivor, a sister, a girl, a granddaughter, a cousin, and a companion.

"My companions and I generally mess around and say 'I contain hoards' the point at which somebody figures out something about us they hadn't expected, yet all the same it's valid: We as a whole contain hoards. For my purposes, being a lady in 2020 isn't feeling embarrassed I frustrated [a person's] assumptions and on second thought acting shocked they didn't expect I was a three-layered individual with more than one story circular segment." — Brooke Knisley

'It's tied in with tackling unimaginable issues'
"I'm the offspring of migrants, fat, strange, and live with chemical imbalance and psychological wellness issues including a dietary problem. Progressively, being a lady in 2020 is [about] tackling unimaginable issues. It is protected yet associated and wanted to Ensure my local area. It's about limits, particularly as a psychological well-being proficient — giving individuals support without transforming every one of my fellowships and connections into remedial ones. It's tied in with being defenseless areas of strength for and, not having every one of the responses." — Alicia Raimundo

'It is completely boss' to 'Be a lady's
"Being a lady is a truly intriguing involvement in regards to the cutting edge age (and all through history, we should be real)... I feel that for me, a player in being a lady implies defending the qualities that I hold, and attempting to ensure that the ladies in general, even and perhaps particularly the people who may not

cross with my life, can carry on with their lives in the manner they decide to.

"Past the worldwide methodology of being a lady, I believe being a lady is completely boss. Ladies are strong, and wonderful, and solid, and uplifting, stunning, amazing, history-producers, and very, truly cool." — Feline Wheeler

'My reality is a demonstration of opposition'
"I would agree that that as a lady of variety, my reality is a demonstration of opposition. Anything I do, regardless of whether I maintain that it should be, is innately political. I explore the world knowing these things...[and] whenever I have an amazing chance to utilize any honor I have for 'good,' I make the most of that.

"As far as I might be concerned, my occupation as an essayist on a Program [The Pleased Family] about a dark family is a tremendous obligation. My work in the day is a ton of pitching jokes, yet I didn't decide to do it since I needed to pitch jokes day in and day out. It was an obligation regarding me to make portrayal on the planet. All that I do is driven by the information that portrayal matters and having a place matters, and that everybody ought to reserve the privilege to have a place." — Ashley Soto

'You can't place me in a little box'

"I was taken on from Vietnam when I was four, and my entire family is white and we live in a town that is under 4,000 individuals and dominantly white. Growing up, I was the main non-white individual or Asian individual at my school. It was similar to a shock to everybody for me to be there... On the off chance that you hadn't seen me and just saw my name and that I'm from Mississippi, you could believe I'm simply a white lady, however you'd always be unable to think about what's behind the name.

"So I believe being a lady in 2020 is breaking that large number of generalizations and not being what everybody anticipates that a lady should be. As somebody who recognizes as so many things, you can't place me in a little box that others could think 'Goodness she's either.' I'm a complex individual. That is the very thing we all are as ladies in 2020, we as a whole are so unique in relation to what a lady could have been during the 1940s or 1950s when they were supposed to be a certain something, whether it's a Chief, an educator, a mother. Regardless of whether you simply need to be a mother to a fuzzy friend, we can gladly be anything we desire." — Sarah Barrett

'Ladies are searching internally now like never before'

"Being a lady to me in 2020 methods mindfulness. I trust the increase in variety concerning orientation character, sexuality, and individual personality is coming from an ascent in mindfulness. Ladies are searching internally more now than any time in recent memory and examining all parts of their character.

"I attempt to be all around as mindful as conceivable with decisive reasoning — I fundamentally attempt to scrutinize the explanation for why I do everything. For what reason am I responding along these lines? For what reason does this fulfill me? For what reason do I think often about this? By posing myself these inquiries I frequently shock myself with the responses, since we never fully acknowledge the amount of our viewpoints and convictions are more subliminal than not.

"With that mindfulness comes certainty — nobody can see you what you are or what you are not on the grounds that you've profoundly investigated that and had those discussions with yourself. That certainty allows us to be secure in our character, yet in addition secure in changing that recognizable proof assuming it feels ideal for us. Being a lady in 2020 is really anything that we want it to be!" — Gabby Beckford

'I'm guaranteeing responsibility for body and my personality'
"Being an eccentric fem-me lady has genuinely been fascinating to explore... Before I had a superior comprehension of my sexuality, I was reluctant to dress less ladylike on the grounds that I figured individuals would think I was eccentric, which is simply my own incorporated homophobia talking. Now that I'm more OK with my character, I view at garments as a creative articulation of who I'm as opposed to something to fear.

"Being a lady implies guaranteeing responsibility for body and my character, upholding for equivalent freedoms for everybody, and ensuring ladies hold the privileges to their bodies. Being a lady causes me to feel like I can be whoever I need to be and would anything that I like to do, whether or not anybody says something else. Being a lady implies strengthening of both myself and different ladies." — Sloan Pecchi

'It's both a superb and perilous thing to be'
"To be a lady in 2020 is both a superb and perilous thing to be. Society is beginning to pay attention to what had been disregarded before: Ladies are being exploited, ladies are being paid less for similar work, ladies are not viewed as proficient pioneers. Nonetheless, the real change that accompanies affirmation appears to be extremely sluggish and disappointing...

"My character [as a Jewish woman] has certainly changed. In the last part of the '90s when I was planning for my Bat Mitzvah, I needed to have a 'exceptionally extraordinary talk' with the rabbi's significant other about what being a lady implied. It was made sense of for me that the ideal lady is an assistance mate to her better half in every way, and was placed on this planet to support the future. This, alongside other comparable encounters, drove me to be less associated with my Judaism. Presently, notwithstanding, with the approach of web-based entertainment, I wind up becoming reconnected to my legacy. On Twitter alone, I follow an extreme rabbi, a rabbi who is a handicap lobbyist, and a Southern rabbi of variety, also the astounding non-twofold, strange, and trans Jews who have woken me up to the numerous ways one can be a Jewish lady." — Aviva Levin

'Being a lady implies being safe and proud'
"Being a lady is the primary thing I relate to. Ladies' privileges, strengthening, and correspondence are the issues that make my head spin with rage and that I'll fight constantly for. I'm additionally Latina and the little girl of a worker, which is likewise a critical part of my personality...

"Being a solitary, 30-year-old, free lady in 2020 to me implies being safe and proud. I'm thankful for my predecessors who prepared to permit me the opportunities I appreciate today, yet know that worldwide, ladies have far to go before we accomplish value and balance in the public eye, at work, and at home." — Lola Méndez

NB: These meetings have been altered and dense for lucidity.

Emma Gannon
London

"I assume I originally felt like a lady when I first appropriately gone to bat for myself. Growing up I was very shaky in my perspectives and trusted others' considerations over my own. Whenever I first thought, Well, that isn't alright, and I will take care of business, was the point at which I felt like a lady. Since ladies are strong AF.

"To me [being a woman] implies being both women's activist and ladylike. It implies occupying room. Some of the time it implies communicating my thoughts wearing astounding beautiful garments and strong make-up and realizing that an interest in magnificence and style doesn't briefly limit my astuteness. I guess a decent beginning stage [to how I figured out how to be a woman] was perusing How to Be a Lady by Caitlin Moran. I read that book when I was 21, and it was the initial step to waking up. We as a whole have various definitions, so I assume I just sorted out my own definition from simply traveling through the world. Being a lady, sadly, implies waiting be hyper-turned on to how the world presently works since it's generally expected not swung in support of ourselves — and it's more terrible for ladies of variety."

CHAPTER ONE

Understanding Being A Lady

The social develop of orientation begins before we are even conceived. It is normal for anticipating that guardians should hypothesize over the sex of their child on the way. A few guardians even toss festivities to uncover the normal orientation of their child. This starts a pattern of gendered assumptions in any event, for the infant, similar to pink or blue extras relying upon the related sex. These doubles can go on as the youngster progresses in years. It appears as young men just getting to play with trucks and young ladies with dolls. For some individuals, they are constrained into either, with regards to what side interests, attributes, and ways of behaving are alloted and anticipated from them. Be that as it may, on the off chance that we glance back at history, it seems to be orientation has been a fluctuating idea. Blue and pink have not forever been divided between the genders and previously, young men even wore dresses until they were six or seven. Since forever ago, various qualities have been divided between the two genders with next to no genuine outcome or reality to what somebody might need to communicate as their orientation.

Making A Day to day existence You Love

Being a lady changes for each lady. Each lady, from a lifelong lady to a mother, holds an alternate response, as our particular discernment and assumptions fluctuate in light of our character and culture. For ladies conceived female (cis ladies) or ladies conceived differently (trans ladies), orientation is something profoundly private and changes in articulation and personality inside womanhood. Anything that your womanhood might seem to be, finding balance in one's life and the standard will prompt generally prosperity and fulfillment throughout everyday life. Giving due consideration to one's well being and health, comprehensively including one's taking care of oneself techniques, and the viability with which one carries out them, can assist you with feeling more comfortable in your body. Making your life into the quirky masterpiece that it normally is takes coordinated consideration, incorporating a harmony between mental, profound and self-awareness.

Whether you are considering your life a lady in the physical, mental, or natural terms, it can really mean something else to every last one of us ladies. Naturally, females fluctuate from guys, both in the regenerative sense and the neurological, compound sense, in spite of the fact that, obviously, not all females can conceive an offspring nor do all ladies have a similar cerebrum science. Ladies have various chemicals, feelings, considerations, and, surprisingly, unique well being concerns and life expectancy. Numerous ladies will confront different well being worries than their male partners, similar to worries over contraception and regenerative well being.

Orientation Separation and Different Peculiarities

In spite of the year, ladies (counting and particularly trans women) appear to be placed in an unexpected section in comparison to men in numerous ways that limit what ladies can be and accomplish. This frequently shows expertly across enterprises in ladies not being advanced as frequently or experiencing issues gaining appreciation in the work environment. White ladies actually make just 79 pennies to a white man's dollar. For ladies of variety, the change rate is surprisingly more dreadful. A Latina lady just makes 55 pennies to a white man's dollar. In any event, for superstars and high-profile ladies, they actually acquire not exactly their male partners.

It wasn't so much that that quite a while in the past that ladies were not even permitted to work, vote, or go to class. It was only after 1971 that the Equivalent Freedoms Revision was supported, and it required an additional eight years and a few additional changes to get the regulations to rise to out like they are today. In any case, despite the fact that the law says that ladies and men are equivalent, persuading the world to act in like manner is a difficult, complex story.

For the vast majority small kids, the standards around orientation articulation and character can confound. Offspring, everything being equal, can appreciate trains, fire engines, Barbie dolls, and tea sets. As a rule the grown-ups in their oversight have a sharp effect between who is permitted to appreciate what.

Since, in truth, there is no great explanation for these things other than generalizing and restricting ways of behaving individuals have seen as perilous, for whatever obsolete explanation.

We have lived in this restricted manner for such a long time that it has turned into a standard and it appears to be that defying this norm will make you "unique." For some individuals, it becomes testing, frightening or even hazardous to seek after the things they maintain that should do or be assuming that they are outside their orientation's apparent assumptions. It is more secure in numerous families and region of the world to mix in with the others and not catch everyone's eye. Nonetheless, there are places and individuals who comprehend that denying yourself the things your spirit needs isn't good for you intellectually. The idea of orientation is social in nature, however that doesn't mean it tends to be disregarded. Everybody should pick whether to acknowledge or face their normal orientation personality and show, regardless of whether they do so intentionally.

What Are Your Life Proclamations?

Everybody has an alternate way of thinking that they carry on with their life by, regardless of whether they are not be guaranteed to in contact with what the principles are expressly. Your life explanations ought to envelop and mirror your own and proficient qualities, filling in as generally an unavoidable vision for progress and individual arrangement. Vision sheets can assist with giving discernible heading to your longings and any overall subjects that could introduce themselves. Your life vision is basically the thing you are needing from your life over the long haul and every one of the little minutes and ways of behaving that will make up your regular routine. This interaction is something that takes a ton of thoughtfulness and coordinated consideration. This life proclamation can assist you with understanding where your orientation will fit in and furthermore, maybe, how it could introduce explicit impediments. Going down a way of opposition doesn't need to be avoided in the event that it is OK for you to do as such.

While people can have comparative sorts of life dreams, it is normal for ladies to feel like they need to act inside a different arrangement of rules and principles. As ladies are capable increasingly more to seek after productive, fruitful professions, numerous ladies are either kept to in any case be moms or homemakers or expected to be both immediately without requesting help. As orientation advances and we extend our thoughts of what anybody is prepared to do, ideally there will be more space for adaptability inside manliness too. Adaptability and space to communicate your thoughts the manner in which you need and need to benefits individuals, all things considered.

The Components of Following Your Insights:

The mind is a muscle and the more you participate in conduct after some time, the simpler it becomes to do. Such are your propensities, as you accomplish something consistently. After some time, a propensity takes less physical and mental energy to finish. Utilizing an organizer or schedule to keep a rundown of what you really want to finish, assisting you with knowing precisely exact thing you want to achieve and permit you to focus on your tasks in view of their significance, serves to intellectually coordinate the things that need to finish.

For instance, on the off chance that you are attempting to eat along specific well being rules or be more dynamic, assuming you work out on your schedule little tokens of these objectives and what you really want to achieve on a miniature size, you have separated an enormous venture into an edible day to day task. This idea likewise stretches out in approaches to counting your undertakings, for example, dinner arranging or keeping a food journal.

Why Such countless Legendary Beasts Are Female
Another assortment of expositions thinks about how the awful ladies of traditional vestige reverberate in contemporary Western culture

Beasts uncover surprisingly about people. As inventions of the creative mind, the outsider, frightening little animal, fanged, winged and in any case unnerving animals that populate fantasies have long assisted social orders with characterizing social limits and answer a well established question: What considers human, and what considers immense?

In the traditional Greek and Roman fantasies that swarm Western legend today, a maybe astounding number of these animals are coded as ladies. These lowlifes, composed classicist Debbie Felton in a 2013 paper, "all addressed men's feeling of dread toward ladies' horrendous potential. The legends then, partially, satisfy a male dream of vanquishing and controlling the female."

Antiquated male creators engraved their feeling of dread toward —
and craving for — ladies into stories about huge females: In his
first-century A.D. incredible Transformations, for instance, the
Roman writer Ovid expounded on Medusa, a startling Gorgon
whose serpentine braids transformed any individual who met her
look into stone. Prior, in Homer's Odyssey, formed around the
seventh or eighth century B.C., the Greek legend Odysseus should
pick between battling Scylla, a six-headed, twelve-legged yapping
animal, and Charybdis, an ocean beast of destruction. Both are
depicted as unambiguously female.

These accounts might sound fantastical today, yet for old
individuals, they mirrored a "semi verifiable" reality, a lost past in
which people lived close by legends, divine beings and the
heavenly, as guardian Madeleine Glennon composed for the
Metropolitan Historical center of Craftsmanship in 2017. Also, the
stories' female beasts uncover more about the male centric
imperatives put on womanhood than they do about ladies
themselves. Medusa struck dread into old hearts since she was both
misleading delightful and revoltingly monstrous; Charybdis scared
Odysseus and his men since she addressed a beating pit of
unlimited craving.

Female beasts address "the sleep time stories male centric society tells itself," supporting assumptions regarding ladies' bodies and conduct, contends columnist and pundit Jess Zimmerman in Ladies and Different Beasts: Building Another Folklore. In this paper assortment, recently distributed by Signal Press, she reconsiders the beasts of days of yore through a women's activist focal point. "Ladies have been beasts, and beasts have been ladies, in hundreds of years of stories," she notes in the book, "since stories are a method for encoding these assumptions and pass them on."

A folklore fan raised on D'Aulaires Book of Greek Legends, Zimmerman composes individual expositions that mix scholarly examination with journal to consider every beast as a lengthy illustration for the assumptions put on ladies right now. She depends on the interpretations and exploration of different works of art researchers, including "beast hypothesis" master Jeffrey Jerome Cohen, Debbie Felton on monster in the antiquated world, Kiki Karoglou's examination of Medusa, Robert E. Ringer's Ladies of Exemplary Folklore and Marianne Hopman on Scylla. Zimmerman likewise joins the positions of other contemporary scholars who have innovatively reconsidered the meaning of these colossal ladies — for example, Muriel Rukeyser, who composed verse about the Sphinx; Margaret Atwood, who retold the tale of Odysseus' better half, Penelope; and Madeline Mill operator, who wrote a 2018 novel about the Greek magician Circe.

However fearsome female beasts spring up in social practices around the world, Zimmerman decided to zero in on antiquated Greek and Roman vestige, which have been dazzled on American culture for ages. "Greek folklore [had] a weighty, weighty impact on Renaissance writing, and craftsmanship and Renaissance writing [have] a weighty effect on our thoughts now, about what comprises scholarly quality, from a really white, cis[gendered], male viewpoint," she makes sense of in a meeting.

Beneath, investigate how the fantasies behind six "horrendous" beasts, from the omniscient Sphinx to the fire-breathing Delusion and the less popular shape shifter Lamia, can enlighten issues in current woman's rights. Zimmerman's book takes a broad perspective of these accounts and their set of experiences, connecting the old past to current governmental issues. According to she, "My expectation is that when you truly do return to the first texts to peruse these accounts, you can contemplate, 'What is this story attempting to give to me?'"

She likewise contends that the characteristics that noticeable these female animals as "massive" to antiquated eyes could have really been their most noteworthy assets. Consider the possibility that, rather than dreading these antiquated beasts, contemporary per users embraced them as legends by their own doing. "The attributes the [monsters] address — yearning, information, strength, want — are not revolting," Zimmerman composes. "In men's grasp, they have forever been gallant."

Scylla and Charybdis

As Homer's Odysseus and his men endeavor to cruise back home to Ithaca, they should go through a restricted, hazardous channel loaded with risk on the two sides. Scylla — a six-headed, twelve-legged animal with necks that stretch out to horrendous lengths and wolf-like heads that grab and eat clueless mariners — lives in a clifftop cave. On the opposite side of the waterway, the sea beast Charybdis seethes and takes steps to suffocate the whole boat.

This sets of beasts, Scylla and Charybdis, intrigued Zimmerman in light of the fact that "they're addressed as things that Odysseus simply needs to move beyond," she says. "So they become piece of his courageous story. However, certainly that is not their main reason? Or possibly, it doesn't need to be their main reason."

Homer depicted Scylla as a beast with few human qualities. However, in Ovid's retelling, expounded on 700 years after the fact, Circe, in an envious angry outburst, transforms Scylla's legs into a squirming mass of woofing canines. As Zimmerman brings up in

Ladies and Different Beasts, what makes Scylla shocking in this variant of the story is "the difference between her wonderful face and her enormous nethers" — a similitude, she contends, for the disdain and dread with which male-ruled social orders respect ladies' bodies when they act in boisterous ways.

Concerning Charybdis, the second-century B.C. Greek student of history Polybius initially recommended that the beast could have related to a geographic reality — a whirlpool that undermined genuine mariners along the Waterway of Messina. In the Odyssey, the Greek legend scarcely gets away from her grasp by sticking to the fragmented remaining parts of his boat.

"[V]oraciousness is [Charybdis'] weapon and her gift," Zimmerman composes, proposing another dynamic of the story. "What strength the proudly ravenous beast courageous woman could have: enough to swallow a man."

Lamia

A 1909 work of art of Lamia by craftsman John William Waterhouse

A 1909 work of art of Lamia by craftsman John William Waterhouse Public space through Wikimedia House

Lamia, one of the less popular evil spirits of traditional folklore, is somewhat of a shapeshifter. She shows up in Greek writer Aristophanes' fifth-century B.C. satire Harmony, then everything except evaporates prior to reappearing in seventeenth and eighteenth century European writing, most remarkably the Heartfelt verse of John Keats.

A few stories hold that Lamia has the chest area of a lady however the lower half of a snake; her name in old Greek makes an interpretation of generally to "rebel shark." Different stories address her as a lady with paws, scales and male genitalia, or even as a multitude of numerous vampiric beasts. Notwithstanding which account one peruses, Lamia's essential bad habit continues as before: She takes and eats youngsters.

Lamia is propelled by sadness; her kids, fathered by Zeus, are killed by Hera, Zeus' better half, in one more fanciful provoke of fury. In her distress, Lamia culls out her own eyes and meanders looking for others' kids; in some retellings, Zeus provides her the capacity to take out her own eyes and set them back freely. (Like Lamia's history, the purposes behind this gift shift from one story to the next. One conceivable clarification, as indicated by Zimmerman, is that Zeus offers this as a little demonstration of leniency toward Lamia, who can't quit imagining her dead youngsters.)

Zimmerman sets that Lamia addresses a firmly established dread about the dangers ladies posture to kids in their culturally recommended jobs as essential guardians. As Felton wrote in 2013, "That ladies could likewise at times produce kids with actual irregularities simply added to the impression of ladies as possibly unnerving and horrendous."

Ladies are supposed to really focus on youngsters, yet society remains "continually stressed [they] will bomb in their commitment to be moms and to be nurturers," Zimmerman says. In the event that a lady rejects parenthood, communicates uncertainty about parenthood, cherishes her kid excessively or loves them excessively little, these demonstrations are seen as infringement, yet to changing degrees.

"To stray in any capacity from the endorsed parenthood story is to be made a beast, a destroyer of kids," Zimmerman composes.

Furthermore, this dread wasn't restricted to Greek stories: La Llorona in Latin America, Penanggalan in Malaysia and Lamashtu in Mesopotamia all took kids also.

Medusa

Like most legendary beasts, Medusa meets her end because of a male legend. Perseus figures out how to kill her, yet just with the guide of a huge number of overwhelmed instruments: winged shoes from courier god Hermes; a cap of imperceptibility from the lord of the hidden world, Abbadon; and a mirror-like safeguard from the goddess of insight and war, Athena.

He really wanted all the support he could assemble. As one of the Gorgons, a threesome of winged ladies with venomous snakes for hair, Medusa positioned among the most dreaded, strong beasts to overwhelm early Greek folklore. In certain renditions of their history, the sisters plunged from Gaia, the representation of Earth herself. Anybody who looked them in the face would go to stone.

Of the three, Medusa was the main human Gorgon. In Ovid's telling, she was once a wonderful lady. Yet, after Poseidon, the lord of the ocean, assaulted her in the sanctuary of Athena, the goddess looked for retribution for what she saw as a demonstration of contamination. As opposed to rebuffing Poseidon, Athena changed his casualty, Medusa, into a revolting beast.

Curiously, imaginative portrayals of Medusa changed decisively over the long haul, turning out to be progressively gendered, said

Karaglou, keeper of the Met display "Hazardous Magnificence: Medusa in Old style Craftsmanship," in a 2018 meeting. In the show, Karaglou joined in excess of 60 portrayals of Medusa's face. Models of the beast from the old fashioned Greek time frame, about 700 to 480 B.C., are for the most part gender ambiguous figures. Intended to be monstrous and compromising, they gloat stubbles, tusks and scowls.

Quick forward to later hundreds of years, and sculptures of Medusa become significantly more conspicuously gorgeous. "Magnificence, similar to monster, captivates, and female excellence specifically was seen — and, somewhat, is as yet seen — to be both charming and perilous, or even lethal," composed Karaglou in a 2018 paper. As the hundreds of years advanced, Medusa's deceptive excellence became inseparable from the peril she presented, establishing the figure of speech of a despicable temptress that perseveres right up 'til now.

Figment

Fabrication, referred to in Hesiod's seventh-century B.C. Theogony and highlighted in Homer's the Iliad, was a tremendous tangle of unique parts: a lion in front, a goat in the center, and a mythical beast or snake on the end. She inhaled fire, flew and assaulted defenseless towns. Specifically, she threatened Lycia, an old sea locale in what is currently southwest Turkey, until the legend Bellerophon figured out how to stop a lead-tipped stick in her throat and gag her to death.

Of the multitude of fictitious beasts, Figment might have had the most grounded establishes actually. A few later students of history, including Pliny the Senior, contend that her story is an illustration of a "euhemerism," when old legend could have compared to verifiable truth. For Fabrication's situation, individuals of Lycia might have been motivated by neighboring topographical movement at Mount Delusion, a geothermal dynamic region where methane gas lights and leaks through breaks in the stones, making little eruptions of flares.

"You can go clear out there today, and individuals heat up their tea on top of these little sprays of geographical action," Zimmerman says.

For old Greeks who recounted the beast, Delusion's specific association of perilous monsters and the homegrown goat addressed a mixture, disconnected loathsomeness that reflected how ladies were seen as the two images of family life and expected dangers. On one hand, composes Zimmerman, Figment's goat body "worries about every one of the concerns of the home, safeguards children … and takes care of them from her body." On the other, her immense components "thunder and cry and inhale fire."

She adds, "What [the goat] adds isn't new strength, however one more sort of fearlessness: the apprehension about the final, of the capricious."

Figment's legend demonstrated so persuasive that it even saturated present day language: In established researchers, "fabrication" presently alludes to any animal with two arrangements of DNA. All the more for the most part, the term alludes to a fantastical invention of somebody's creative mind.

The Sphinx

One of the most conspicuous goliaths of times long past, the Sphinx was a figure famous across Egypt, Asia and Greece. A half breed of different animals, the legendary being expected various implications in every one of these societies. In old Egypt, for example, the 66-foot-tall lion-bodied sculpture that monitors the Incomparable Pyramid of Giza was probable male and planned, likewise, as a male image of force.

Across the Mediterranean, writer Sophocles composed the Sphinx into his fifth-century B.C. misfortune Oedipus Rex as a female beast with the body of a feline, the wings of a bird, and a premonition repository of intelligence and questions. She goes to Thebes from unfamiliar grounds and eats up anybody who can't accurately answer her conundrum: What goes on four legs in the first part of the day, two feet around early afternoon and three PM? (Reply: a man, who creeps as a child, strolls as a grown-up and involves a stick as a senior.)

At the point when Oedipus effectively finishes her riddle, the Sphinx is upset to such an extent that she hurls herself to her demise. This, Zimmerman composes, is the obvious end result for a culture that rebuffed individuals for hushing up about information. Information is power — that is the reason in present day history, Zimmerman contends, men have barred ladies from admittance to formal schooling.

"The narrative of the Sphinx is the tale of a lady with questions men can't respond to," she composes. "Men required that somewhat worse in the fifth century [B.C.] than they do now."

CHAPTER TWO

Is child birth a plaque to women

Each second, around 4.3 births happen all through the world. A few births give joy, others bitterness. Many are needed, numerous undesirable. Most infants are naturally introduced to destitution, a couple into riches. Anything that the conditions, those conceiving an offspring know and feel its significance. The people who notice birth, whether they are a maternity specialist, sage-femme, birth chaperon, accomplice, companion, family or outsider, realize they have been essential for an interaction that guarantees our species proceeding with presence and embodies human substance.

It means quite a bit to Be conceived

You who have remained at the bedposts

What's more, seen a mother on her high collect day,

The day of the most brilliant of gather moons for her.

You who have seen the new wet kid

Dried behind the ears,

Wrapped up in delicate new article of clothing,

Tightening its lips and sending a grabbing mouth

Toward areolas where white milk is prepared.

You who have seen loves payday

Of wild ringing and sweet anguishing.

You know being conceived is significant
You know that nothing else meant a lot to you
You comprehend that the payday of adoration is so old,
So involved, so followed with the circles of the moon,
So clever with the mysteries of the salts of the blood
It should be more seasoned than the moon, more seasoned than salt.

It Means quite a bit to Be Conceived
Carl Sandburg

Birth has been addressed by people since pr-noteworthy times in verse, exposition, drawing, painting, form, film, video, photography, theater, materials, web-based entertainment, music and every other human articulation under the sun. Through each such portrayal we endeavor to convey and observe meaning. Maternity specialists and maternity care understudies can gain proficiency with an extraordinary arrangement about birth's implications all over the planet by drawing in with the numerous human imaginative articulations around birth that they will experience. It is vital to know that every individual's one of a kind point of view impacts how they answer portrayals around labor and how they quality significance. These contrasting viewpoints impact the author, craftsman, or picture taker who produces curios as well as the individuals who see the work. Barbara Bolt in her book Craftsmanship Past Portrayal helps us that the demonstration to remember making the work is performative and that perspective should be viewed as notwithstanding the completed work. Burton in her book Natal Signs, looks at the structure of Michel de Certau and brings up that the boundary isolating creation and utilization is permeable; the purchaser of any work is unavoidably taken part in a type of optional creation. As birthing specialists, we should know that our remarkable understandings are given to our clients, our networks and at last to our strategy producers.

While drawing in with portrayals of labor, it is fundamental to think about the substance of the work as well as the way things are utilized and for what reason. Is craftsmanship political? This discussion has existed in the craftsmanship world for quite a while. Assuming being political means drawing in with endlessly power connections - whether that is the association between subjects in the work, among craftsman and subject, among craftsman and craftsman - then, at that point, yes all workmanship is political. Power is implanted in the regular; the manner in which all that in the public arena works. It is basic to look at how portrayals question power relations, 'disrupt suspicions, and break limits.' The more work done in attempting to comprehend viewpoints of the people who expound on labor from an individual, verifiable or anthropological system, make craftsmanship or verse, the better birthing specialists will actually want to accompany 'lady.'

In any case, nobody can 'know' how others have or will encounter labor. So how might an understudy of maternity care, in this time, here, grasp the mind boggling convergence of physiology and culture? How might anybody examine what labor resembled quite a while back in Mesopotamia or even how it affects the lady looking for maternity care today?

This part will furnish a chance to draw in with portrayals of birth and its importance. In noticing works, numerous craftsmanship history specialists underscore the connection between the stylish, the tactile or close to home estimations evoked, as well as the expectation or perusing of the work. To be available while looking or potentially paying attention to portrayals of labor, includes posing inquiries about the work that investigate these connections. In every one of the accompanying segments, there are various inquiries to assist you with considering the included portrayals. A work might make us stop, look or listen cautiously, feel moved, experience bliss or pity. We might have the option to say we like or aversion a piece of workmanship or sonnet or comic but be uncertain why that is so. Frequently, we really want to take a gander at a craftsmanship piece a few times or ponder a work of fiction or verse over the long haul before we grasp our response to it.

Portrayals OF BIRTH Since forever ago

Despite the fact that pregnancy, birth and parenthood/life as a parent have been subjects of conversation and portrayal by people for millennia, this segment will examine four specific periods in history that delineated the significance and importance of birth in their time in very various ways.

EARLY Portrayals OF Ripeness and BIRTH

We have proof that types of early people were making two and three-layered pictures a long time back. Cavern artistic creations of creatures and human hands dating to 35,000BCE have been tracked down on the island of Sulawesi in Indonesia. Who painted them, their sentiments, contemplation s related with the work, why they were painted, and the implications they had at the time are undeniably lost to history. Nonetheless, importance turns out to be fairly more clear when we notice three-layered figures that seem to address richness and birth. 'Venus dolls' is a term used to depict little, somewhere in the range of two and eight inches (5-20cm), models of ladies. Albeit etched during the pr-memorable period, the term Venus was all the more as of late applied by archeologist s to reflect Venus, the Roman goddess of magnificence. These figures are typically comparative in size, showing up completely fleshed with huge stomachs and bosoms, and minimal facial detail. Archeologist s banter whether these little figures address ripeness or are a strict image of the time.

One of the most well known of these is the Venus of Willendorf, or Lady of Willendorf, named for the Austrian town wherein it was found in 1908. The 11 cm high statuette is assessed to have been made somewhere in the range of 24,000 and 22,000 BCE. She is convincing a result of her enormous size, which would be called large today. The fact that her curve infers fruitfulness makes it guessed by numerous.

One more type of creative portrayals of richness and birth is tracked down in early mats from Turkey, Kurdish floor coverings, Qashqai, Lori, and Shah Savan carpets of Iran and the Balusch and Turkoman mats of Focal Asia. All have a theme that has been depicted as a ripeness/birth image, an improved on visual communication of a pregnant female, representing a reverence of birth and age of life. There are numerous images from numerous practices that represent fruitfulness and labor in floor coverings and materials, and similarly as numerous material experts who say it is challenging to decipher the importance of images created millennia prior. In any case the richness/birth image in materials has a few normal qualities that have been depicted: a focal jewel, sitting spot on, with sets of bended or snared lines projecting from the top and base places . The precious stone addresses the body of the pregnant lady and the lines her arms and legs. In certain forms, a little jewel sits inside the bigger one or the theme is extended with additional snared or bended lines.

BIRTH IN RENAISSANCE EUROPE (Fourteenth TO THE Seventeenth Hundreds of years)

In the hour of the Renaissance, in post-plague Europe, the physiology of labor had not been all around examined, and very little had been expounded on it. Birthing was ladies' work, it was private, and it was hazardous given the high paces of maternal and newborn child mortality. Birth, albeit hazardous, was commended and elaborate arrangements were started a very long time before the child was expected. The genuine apprehensions around labor brought about an overflow of things that could give security or potentially intervention around the course of propagation. Charms, birth plate , and compositions were much of the time showed in the home in the desire for guaranteeing great birthing results for mother and child.

Ladies were urged to take a gander at lovely pictures, specifically photos of the pregnant Madonna, the Introduction of the Virgin, or the Introduction of Holy person John the Baptist so they could envision themselves having an effective birth and sound child like the subjects of the canvases. The works of art and birth plate portrayed the period following birth at home; an exceptionally suitable environment with the lady encompassed by maternity specialists and companions. There are frequently upwards of ten ladies in the portrayals of birth. The specialists portrayed their subjects in story structure so the works of art uncover the exercises that could have occurred over a time of days. The ladies are completely dressed in the dress style of the day and there is no sign of the chaos of birth. A typical visual component in the canvases is a female partner conveying food and drink into the room on a wooden plate after the birth.

Hand painted birth plate were a typical gift to a recently hitched couple, and were intended to be gone on through ages. On one side of the plate there was in many cases a birth scene and on the other a canvas of a child kid. Likewise with compositions of effective births, it was trusted that assuming the lady was encircled by, and zeroed in on, pictures of child young men, she would deliver a male kid and a lady's worth was many times estimated by her capacity to create a kid.

Despite the fact that demise was normal during the fourteenth seventeenth 100 years, and numerous funerary landmarks worked, there were not many burial chambers respecting ladies and explicitly ladies who passed on in labor. As a matter of fact there is only one 'contemporary Western portrayal of death in child-bed, whether in obstetrical texts, sacrosanct or common compositions, or great craftsmanship and that is the cut help of the passing of Francesca Tornabouni, encompassed by her birthing specialist and chaperons. It was finished by Andrea Verrocchio in 1477, and is presently situated in the Bargello Exhibition hall in Florence. Francesca's significant other, Giovanni, supported this one of a kind landmark as a presentation of his commitment and pain. Note the restless looks and arm and body developments of the orderlies The Italian craftsman Francesco Furini (mid seventeenth 100 years) painted a labor passing scene from the Jewish Book of scriptures story of Jacob and Rachel, named The Introduction of Benjamin and the Demise of Rachel . This painting is like the Tornabuoni help in that Rachel is encircled by her birthing specialist orderlies, her body is stooped over like that of Francesca Tornabuoni and the chaperons have restless looks and tense body positions. Visual portrayals of death in labor are uncommon today however labor passings are all the more normally portrayed in writing

LATE Nineteenth 100 years, Mid Twentieth CENTURY Ladies Craftsmen AND BIRTH

Craftsmanship by ladies started to be viewed in a serious way by workmanship history specialists and society in the late nineteenth hundred years. Before that time, it was challenging for ladies to acquire sufficient preparation and earn proficient respect and status practically identical to men. Subsequently, a large number of the previous portrayals of the birth room and its numerous female orderlies were made by male craftsmen in view of family discussions about the exercises that went on. Pushing ahead to the late nineteenth and mid twentieth Hundred years, ladies were turning out to be more perceived as skillful and gifted craftsmen Pregnancy, in any case, was surprisingly underrepresented in the numerous points addressed in the visual expressions until crafted by Paula Modersohn-Becker, Frida Kahlo and Alice Neel became regarded and ordinary. The craftsmanship history writing is loaded with investigations and scrutinizes of their work. In these works, we feel a closeness; we are eye to eye with the subjects, who as a matter of fact are the specialists in a portion of these works.

PAULA MODERSOHN-BECKER (1876-1907)

Paula Modersohn-Becker was brought up in Germany however moved to France to concentrate on painting at the age of 24. She is viewed as the main female painter to arrange female naked self-pictures. She looks at her own exposed body to 'her spirit uncovered' (11, p.14) in a letter to her better half Otto in 1903. Her bareness then 'turns into a representation for genuineness or transparency's (11, p.14) One of her most notable self-pictures is a picture of herself as a pregnant lady, in spite of the fact that she presently couldn't seem to become pregnant. This painting is quite possibly the earliest illustration of self-portrayal; a canvas about pregnancy by a lady who is envisioning the way that she would look if pregnant.

The canvas, then, is a similitude for how she had an outlook on herself as a youthful craftsman: fertile, ready, capable without precedent for her life to make and paint openly in the way that she wished. What she is going to bring forth isn't a kid however her full grown, free, creative self. Customarily, naked representations of ladies had been painted for the delectation of the male look, however here Paula makes another develop: a lady who can sustain herself outside the features of marriage, who needn't bother with a man to be satisfied.

Modersohn-Becker became pregnant at the age of 30, one year subsequent to finishing, Self-Representation on Her 6th Wedding Commemoration. Eighteen days subsequent to bringing forth her girl, Modersohn-Becker passed on from an embolism

ALICE NEEL (1900-1984)

Alice Neel was an American painter known for resisting the shows and governmental issues of the day. Despite the fact that Modersohn-Becker painted delicate and lovely pregnant nudes in the mid 1990's it was only after Neel, in the 1960's that pregnancy was again in the dictionary of specialists. In 1964, after a few loved ones became pregnant Neel started painting her sharp, reasonable, non-heartfelt pregnant nudes. She painted seven pregnant nudes somewhere in the range of 1964 and 1978 and moved toward these compositions and all her representation with a 'knowing and unfazed eye.' Her subjects were ladies she knew, whose accounts were recognizable to her. They are painted gazing straight toward the watcher - which was rather than a significant number of the female nudes in European and Asian craftsmanship who turn away from the watcher and the watcher who maybe has a sensual interest. She needed to paint in resistance of the male look. Regardless, her work on pregnancy was not viewed as a suitable subject by certain women's activists since 'it took steps to give proof to the charge - sure to send ladies back to their rural penitentiaries - that 'life systems is destiny."

Neel, who was a single parent and whose own set of experiences with parenthood is convoluted, came to painting her pregnant nudes when she was past menopause, carrying a distance and viewpoint to the work. Her 1978 composition of Margaret Evans, the spouse of a companion of Neel's, who is conveying twins mirrors Neel's perspective on pregnancy as an unavoidable truth with its bliss and its horror, a condition where ladies are grounded and not available to be purchased.

FRIDA KAHLO, (1907 - 1954)

Kahlo was a Mexican craftsman whose life was overwhelmed by handicap, disease and torment, which are all addressed in her creative work. She was hitched to individual painter Diego Rivera, an adoration that carried both delight and torment to her life. Kahlo especially needed to have kids and became pregnant a few times however the pregnancies each finished in unnatural birth cycle. In this specific circumstance, she painted her experience of a premature delivery while in the US. Unsuccessful labor was not openly discussed during the 1930s; it was a wellspring of disgrace, so her fortitude in painting this point mirrored her need to talk the unspeakable in the manner she knew how.

21ST CENTURY Portrayals

Today, we are immersed with striking depictions of pregnancy and birth. Not just through customary portrayals in craftsmanship, fiction, and verse yet in addition through express pictures truly TV and on the web. The present media permits pregnancy and birth to be given greater intricacy and empowers a more extensive scope of encounters to be addressed than could be previously. Innovation allows us to partake in, rethink and, even reuse portrayals of ordinary birth, convoluted birth, pregnancy and birth with a handicap, LGBTQ2 encounters, pregnancy misfortune, sci-fi and symbol births.

In under 50 years, the depictions of pregnancy and birth have transformed from craftsman's portrayals in text, model and painting to incorporate genuine, clear pictures we see on TV, web journals and sites. Anybody with a web association can watch a video of work and birth from start to finish and view births in medical clinic, at home, a birth community, in water, or in standing, hunching down, or sitting positions. Web-based entertainment stages, for example, Twitter, Instagram and Facebook all work with message, photographs and brief recordings of labor. From a good ways, even as an alien to those that post, we can get a brief look into the implications of birth for those people who post photographs and recordings.

Luce et al., subsequent to investigating a few TV episodes showing births, inferred that due to the allure of 'crisis' births with inconveniences, ladies might enter their own introduction to the world involvement in fears created by what they have seen. Those feelings of trepidation, she proposes, advance the medicalization of birth.

This feeling of dread toward labor has developed as a subject of exploration throughout recent years. Does admittance to bountiful wellsprings of data increment or abatement ladies' feelings of trepidation? A Google search of individual accounts of birth turns up huge number of potential outcomes. How do childbearing clients figure out that data to find, precise data, yet stories from others 'like them'? Assuming that one is poor, socially moderate, strict, what is the effect? Stoll and Corridor in their investigation of north of 4,000 understudies at the College of English Columbia found that 'young ladies whose mentalities toward pregnancy and birth were formed by the media were 1.5 times bound to report labor dread.' European renaissance ladies dreaded labor due to what they didn't have the foggiest idea; today we might fear labor in light of all we do be aware.

Review Alternate Approaches to BEING

The moving scene of portrayals of labor is opening up better approaches for seeing and pondering birth. Just as of late have we seen portrayals of bodies and connections that don't fit the customary ideal. Incapacity, and LGBTQ2 encounters are starting to be portrayed.

Inability EXPERIENCE

People with a handicap have been underestimated in our general public and thusly, they are seldom the subjects of craftsmanship. To some in the public eye, those with handicaps are not intended to be sexual, not to mention be pregnant or a parent. (21) Marc Quinn was one of the first to challenge that view through huge scope design. (22) Quinn has made a few figures of Alison Lapper, while she was pregnant. Lapper is an English craftsman who was brought into the world with phocomelia. Quinn was attracted to Lapper as addressing somebody who defeated her conditions. At the point when she became pregnant she was encouraged to have a fetus removal so her youngster wouldn't turn into a weight to society. She persevered, breastfeed her child kid, took him to school on her wheelchair, battled for inability freedoms, and presently makes money as a craftsman for the Mouth and Foot Painting Specialists. She got a Privileged Doctorate from the College of Brighton in 2014.

Quinn's marble model of Lapper was essential for a pivoting contemporary figure show in Trafalgar Square, London, UK (F, and it openly praised the magnificence of an alternate body. Met with both analysis and commendation, the model asks the watcher to inquiry the tight limits of acknowledged normal practices.

LGBTQ2 Encounters

As of late has the well being writing started to address the pregnancy and childbearing necessities of people who distinguish or present as lesbian, gay, sexually unbiased, transsexual, eccentric or twofold vivacious. Birthing assistance and doula sites in Canada and somewhere else give rules to delicate consideration. A considerable lot of the rules depend on the way of thinking framed by Canadian Relationship of Maternity specialists position proclamation on Orientation Inclusivity and Common freedoms.

The experience of transsexual pregnancy specifically has been depicted in papers and scholarly text. The visual pictures and composed message of Thomas Beatie and Yuval Clincher's pregnancies are instances of portrayals accessible to us as we envision the significance of pregnancy to these men, their families and to society later on. The kickoff of the Exhibition hall of Transsexual History and Workmanship, Chicago and the distribution of realistic books, for example, Pregnant Butch are instances of changes that offer substantial help for the achievements and opportunities for trans-gendered guardians.

Portrayals

We presently live in when portrayals of the body overall and the pregnant body specifically are not generally so compelled by friendly show. This isn't to imply that that numerous portrayals don't bring up issues of morals or social propriety. The most effective method to decipher the blast of portrayals is really difficult for all ladies and guardians. Understanding is affected by the general public we live in. The importance of pregnancy and of birth is formed by the general public every client lives in bringing about extraordinary contrasts in significance between rustic Nunavut in Canada, metropolitan New York City, or the less evolved nation of Sierra Leone. Social orders are molded by how ladies are seen, how sexuality is seen and the job of religion in the general public and the existence of the individual, and every one of these will influence on the importance of birth to a client.

Birth is significant. As ladies have more organization over the statement of portrayals of this groundbreaking occasion, they will actually want to encounter an implying that fills them with sensations of solidarity and solace. Sharon Olds sonnet, The Language of the Gloat, communicates the delight she feels in involving her body in labor while using male symbolism to portray her solidarity and sensation of triumph.

CHAPTER THREE

FEMINISIM

Woman's rights carries numerous things to reasoning including not just different specific moral and political cases, yet approaches to posing and addressing inquiries, helpful and basic exchange with standard philosophical perspectives and strategies, and new subjects of request. Women's activist logicians work inside every one of the significant practices of philosophical grant including insightful way of thinking, American Realist reasoning, and Continental theory. Passages in this Reference book showing up under the heading "woman's rights, approaches" talk about the effect of these practices on women's activist grant and look at the chance and allure of work that makes joins between two customs. Women's activist commitments to and meditations in standard philosophical discussions are shrouded in passages in this reference book under "woman's rights, intercessions". Sections covered under the rubric "women's liberation, points" concern philosophical issues that emerge as women's activists articulate records of sexism, study chauvinist social and social practices, and foster elective dreams of a simply world. To put it plainly, they are philosophical themes that emerge inside women's liberation.

In spite of the fact that there are various and some of the time clashing ways to deal with women's activist way of thinking, it is educational to start by asking what, regardless, women's activists as a gathering are focused on. Taking into account a portion of the discussions over what women's liberation is gives a springboard to perceiving how women's activist responsibilities produce a large group of philosophical subjects, particularly as those responsibilities face the world as far as we might be concerned.

What is Women's liberation?(feminism)

Women's activist Convictions and Women's activist Developments
The term 'women's liberation' has a wide range of purposes and its implications are frequently challenged. For instance, a journalists utilize the term 'woman's rights' to allude to a generally unambiguous political development in the US and Europe; different scholars use it to allude to the conviction that there are treacheries against ladies, however there is no agreement on the specific rundown of these shameful acts. Albeit the expression "woman's rights" has a set of experiences in English connected with ladies' activism from the late nineteenth hundred years to the present, it is helpful to recognize women's activist thoughts or convictions from women's activist political developments, for even in periods where there has been no critical political activism around ladies' subjection, people have been worried about and hypothesized about equity for ladies. Thus, for instance, it's a good idea to find out if Plato was a women's activist, given his view that

ladies ought to be prepared to govern (Republic, Book V), despite the fact that he was an exemption in his authentic setting. (See e.g., Tuana 1994.)

Our objective here isn't to overview the historical backdrop of women's liberation — as a bunch of thoughts or as a progression of political developments — yet rather is to portray a portion of the focal purposes of the term that are generally pertinent to those intrigued by contemporary women's activist way of thinking. The references we give underneath are just a little example of the work accessible on the subjects being referred to; more complete catalogs are accessible at the particular effective sections and furthermore toward the finish of this passage.

During the 1800s the term 'woman's rights' was utilized to allude to "the characteristics of females", and it was only after the Primary Worldwide Ladies' Gathering in Paris in 1892 that the term, following the French expression féministe, was utilized consistently in English for a confidence in and support of equivalent freedoms for ladies in light of the possibility of the balance of the genders. Albeit the expression "woman's rights" in English is pull in the preparation for lady testimonial in Europe and the US during the late nineteenth and mid twentieth 100 years, obviously endeavors to get equity for ladies didn't start or end with this time of activism.[1] So some have found it helpful to consider the ladies' development in the US happening in "waves". On the wave model, the battle to accomplish fundamental political privileges during the period from the mid-nineteenth 100 years until the entry of the Nineteenth Amendment in 1920 considers "First Wave" woman's rights. Woman's rights disappeared between the two universal conflicts, to be "resuscitated" in the last part of the 1960's and mid 1970's as "Second Wave" women's liberation. In this subsequent wave, women's activists pushed past the early journey for political privileges to battle for more noteworthy uniformity no matter how you look at it, e.g., in training, the working environment, and at home. Later changes of women's liberation have come about in a "Third Wave". Third Wave women's activists frequently study Second Wave woman's rights for its absence of consideration regarding the distinctions among ladies because of race, identity, class, ethnicity, religion (see Segment 2.3 underneath; likewise Breines 2002; Spring 2002), and underline "character" as a site of orientation battle. (For more data on the "wave" model and each of the "waves", see Other Web Assets.)

Nonetheless, a few women's activist researchers object to recognizing woman's rights with these specific snapshots of political activism, because doing so obscures the way that there has been protection from male mastery that ought to be thought of "women's activist" since forever ago and across societies: i.e., woman's rights isn't restricted to a couple (White) ladies in the West over the course of the last 100 years or something like that. Besides, in any event, taking into account just generally late endeavors to oppose male control in Europe and the US, the accentuation on "First" and "Second" Wave woman's rights disregards the continuous protection from male mastery between the 1920's and 1960's and the opposition outside standard legislative issues, especially by ladies of variety and common ladies (Cott 1987).

One technique for tackling these issues is distinguish woman's rights as far as a bunch of thoughts or convictions as opposed to support in a specific political development. As we saw over, this likewise enjoys the benefit of permitting us to find secluded women's activists whose work was not perceived or valued during their time. Be that as it may, how might we approach recognizing a center arrangement of women's activist convictions? Some would propose that we ought to zero in on the political thoughts that the term was evidently begat to catch, viz., the obligation to ladies' equivalent privileges. This recognizes that obligation to and support for ladies' privileges has not been bound to the Ladies' Freedom Development in the West. Yet, this also raises discussion, for it outlines woman's rights inside a comprehensively Liberal way to deal with political and financial life. Albeit most women's activists would presumably concur that there is some feeling of "freedoms" on which accomplishing equivalent privileges for ladies is a fundamental condition for woman's rights to succeed, most would likewise contend that this doesn't be sound adequate. This is on the grounds that ladies' persecution under male mastery only very seldom comprises exclusively in denying ladies of political and lawful "freedoms", yet additionally stretches out into the construction of our general public and the substance of our way of life, and saturates our awareness (e.g., Bartky 1990).

Is there any point, then, to asking what women's liberation is? Given the contentions over the term and the legislative issues of surrounding the limits of a social development, it is in some cases enticing to believe that everything we can manage is to verbalize a bunch of disjuncts that catch a scope of women's activist convictions. Nonetheless, simultaneously it tends to be both mentally and politically significant to have a schematic structure that empowers us to plan in any event a portion of our places of understanding and conflict. We'll start here by thinking about a portion of the fundamental components of women's liberation as a political position or set of convictions. For a study of various philosophical ways to deal with women's liberation, see "Woman's rights, ways to deal with".

Regulating and Engaging Parts

In a significant number of its structures, women's liberation appears to include no less than two gatherings of cases, one standardizing and the other engaging. The standardizing claims concern how ladies should (or should not) to be seen and treated and draw on a foundation origination of equity or wide upright position; the graphic cases concern how ladies are, truly, saw and treated, charging that they are not being treated as per the principles of equity or ethical quality conjured in the regulating claims. Together the standardizing and elucidating claims give motivations to attempting to significantly impact the status quo; consequently, woman's rights isn't simply a scholarly yet in addition a political development.

Thus, for instance, a Liberal methodology of the sort previously referenced could characterize women's liberation (rather shortsightedly here) with regards to two cases:

(Regulating) People are qualified for equivalent privileges and regard.

(Enlightening) Ladies are as of now hindered concerning freedoms and regard, contrasted and men [… in such and such regards and because of such and such circumstances…].

On this record, that ladies and men should have equivalent privileges and regard is the standardizing guarantee; and that ladies are denied equivalent freedoms and regard capabilities here as the illustrative case. In fact, the case that ladies are distraught as for privileges and regard is definitely not a "simply engaging" guarantee since it conceivably includes an evaluative part. Nonetheless, our point here is basically that cases of this sort concern what is the case not what should be the situation. Besides, as demonstrated by the ellipsis over, the spellbinding part of a meaningful women's activist view won't be articulable in a solitary case, yet will include a record of the particular social systems that deny ladies of, e.g., privileges and regard. For instance, is the essential wellspring of ladies' subjection her job in the family? (Engels 1845; Okin 1989) Or is it her part in the work market? (Bergmann 2002) Is the issue guys' inclinations to sexual brutality (and what is the wellspring of these propensities?)? (Brownmiller 1975; MacKinnon 1987) Or is it basically ladies' natural job in multiplication? (Firestone 1970)

Conflicts inside women's liberation can happen concerning either the spellbinding or regulating claims, e.g., women's activists vary on what might consider equity or unfairness for ladies (what considers "correspondence," "persecution," "detriment", what freedoms should everybody be agreed?) , and what kinds of foul play ladies truth be told endure (what parts of ladies' ongoing circumstance are hurtful or unreasonable?). Conflicts may likewise lie in the clarifications of the treachery: two women's activists might concur that ladies are unfairly being denied legitimate privileges and regard but meaningfully contrast in their records of how or why the bad form happens and what is expected to end it (Jaggar 1994).

Conflicts among women's activists and non-women's activists can happen as for both the standardizing and unmistakable cases too, e.g., some non-women's activists concur with women's activists on the manners in which ladies should be seen and treated, however see no issue with the manner in which things at present are. Others differ about the foundation moral or political perspectives.

With an end goal to propose a schematic record of woman's rights, Susan James describes women's liberation as follows:

Woman's rights is grounded on the conviction that ladies are persecuted or hindered by examination with men, and that their abuse is here and there ill-conceived or outlandish. Under the umbrella of this overall portrayal there are, notwithstanding, numerous translations of ladies and their persecution, with the goal that it is a misstep to consider woman's rights a solitary philosophical precept, or as suggesting a concurred political program. (James 2000, 576)

James appears to be here to utilize the ideas of "persecution" and "impediment" as placeholders for additional considerable records of foul play (both regularizing and distinct) over which women's activists clash.

Some could like to characterize women's liberation as far as a regularizing guarantee alone: women's activists are the people who accept that ladies are qualified for equivalent privileges, or equivalent regard, or… (fill in the clear with one's favored record of shamefulness), and one isn't expected to accept that ladies are as of now being dealt with unreasonably. Be that as it may, if we somehow managed to take on this phrased show, it would be more earnestly to recognize a portion of the fascinating wellsprings of conflict both with and inside women's liberation, and the term 'woman's rights' would lose quite a bit of its capability to join those whose worries and responsibilities stretch out past their ethical convictions to their social translations and political affiliations. Women's activists are not just the people who are committed on a basic level to equity for ladies; women's activists take themselves to have motivations to achieve social change for ladies' sake.

Taking "woman's rights" to involve both standardizing and experimental responsibilities additionally assists make with detecting of certain purposes of the term 'women's liberation' in late well known talk. In regular discussion it is entirely expected to find all kinds of people prefixing a remark they could make about ladies with the proviso, "I'm not a women's activist, yet… ". Obviously this capability may be (and is) utilized for different purposes, however one tenacious use appears to follow the capability with some case that is difficult to recognize from claims that women's activists are wont to make. E.g., I'm not a women's activist however I accept that ladies ought to procure equivalent compensation for equivalent work; or I'm not a women's activist yet I'm happy that top notch ladies ball players are at long last gaining some appreciation in the WNBA. In the event that we see the ID "women's activist" as verifiably committing one to both a standardizing position about how things ought to be and an understanding of current circumstances, it is not difficult to envision somebody being in the place of needing to drop their underwriting of either the regularizing or the illustrative case. Thus, e.g., one may recognize that there are situations where ladies have been impeded without needing to purchase any wide upright hypothesis that takes a position on things like this (particularly where it is indistinct what that expansive hypothesis is). Or on the other hand one may recognize in an extremely broad manner that uniformity for ladies is something to be thankful for, without being focused on deciphering specific regular circumstances as shameful (particularly on the off chance that is hazy the way in which far these understandings would need to expand). Women's activists, nonetheless, basically as per famous talk, are prepared to both embrace an expansive record of equity for ladies' expectation's and decipher ordinary circumstances as shameful by the principles of that record. The individuals who unequivocally drop their obligation to woman's rights may then be glad to embrace some piece of the view however are reluctant to underwrite what they view as a tricky bundle.

As referenced above, there is impressive discussion inside woman's rights concerning the regularizing question: what might consider (full) equity for ladies? What is the idea of some unacceptable that woman's rights tries to address? E.g., is some unacceptable that ladies have been denied equivalent freedoms? Is it that ladies have been denied equivalent regard for their disparities? Is it that ladies' encounters have been overlooked and depreciated? Is everything of the above mentioned and that's only the tip of the iceberg? What system would it be advisable for us to utilize to recognize and resolve the issues? (It's obvious, e.g., Jaggar 1983; Youthful 1990a; Tuana and Tong 1995.) Women's activist thinkers specifically have inquired: Do the standard philosophical records of equity and ethical quality give us sufficient assets to hypothesize male mastery, or do we want particularly women's activist records? (E.g., Okin 1979; Hoagland 1989; Okin 1989; Ruddick 1989; Benhabib 1992; Hampton 1993; Held 1993; Tong 1993; Baier 1994; Ill humored Adams 1997; Walker 1998; Kittay 1999; Robinson 1999; Youthful 2011; O'Connor 2008).

Note, in any case, that by stating the undertaking as one of recognizing the wrongs ladies endure (and have endured), there is an implied idea that ladies as a gathering can be conveniently contrasted against men collectively and regard to their standing or position in the public eye; and this strongly implies that ladies as a gathering are treated similarly, or that they all experience similar treacheries, and men as a gathering all procure similar benefits. Obviously this isn't true, or possibly not clearly so. As ringer snares so strikingly called attention to, in 1963 when Betty Friedan encouraged ladies to reexamine the job of housewife and requested more prominent open doors for ladies to enter the labor force (Friedan 1963), Friedan was not representing common ladies or most ladies of variety (snares 1984, 1-4). Nor was she representing lesbians. Ladies as a gathering experience various types of treachery, and the sexism they experience communicates in complex ways with different frameworks of mistreatment. In contemporary terms, this is known as the issue of diversity (Crenshaw 1991). This evaluate has driven a few scholars to oppose the mark "woman's rights" and take on an alternate name for their view. Prior, during the 1860s-80s, the term 'womanism' had once in a while been utilized for such savvy and political responsibilities; all the more as of late, Alice Walker has suggested that "womanism" gives a contemporary option in contrast to "woman's rights" that better tends to the necessities of People of color and ladies of variety all the more by and large (Walker 1990).

Woman's rights and the Variety of Ladies

To think about a portion of the various systems for answering the peculiarity of interconnection, we should get back to the schematic cases that ladies are mistreated and this persecution is off-base or out of line. Comprehensively, then, one could portray the objective of woman's rights to end the persecution of ladies. However, in the event that we likewise recognize that ladies are mistreated by sexism, yet in numerous ways, e.g., by inequity, homophobia, prejudice, ageism, ableism, and so forth, then it could appear to be that the objective of woman's rights is to end all persecution that influences ladies. Also, a few women's activists have embraced this translation, e.g., (Product 1970), cited in (Crow 2000, 1).

Note, nonetheless, that not all concur with such a far reaching meaning of woman's rights. One could concur that women's activists should attempt to end all types of mistreatment — persecution is low and women's activists, similar to every other person, have an ethical constraint to battle unfairness — without keeping up with that it is the mission of woman's rights to end all abuse. One could try and trust that to achieve women's liberation's objectives it is important to battle bigotry and financial double-dealing, yet in addition feel that there is a smaller arrangement of explicitly women's activist targets. At the end of the day, contradicting persecution in its many structures might be instrumental to, even a viable way to, women's liberation, however not natural for it. E.g., chime snares contends:

Woman's rights, as freedom battle, should exist separated from and as a piece of the bigger battle to destroy mastery in the entirety of its structures. We should comprehend that man centric control imparts a philosophical establishment to bigotry and different types of gathering abuse, and that there is no expectation that it tends to be killed while these frameworks stay in salvageable shape. This information ought to reliably illuminate the bearing regarding women's activist hypothesis and practice. (snares 1989, 22) For snares, the principal quality that recognizes woman's rights from other freedom battles is its anxiety with sexism:

Dissimilar to numerous women's activist confidants, I accept ladies and men should share a typical comprehension — a fundamental information on what woman's rights is — on the off chance that it is ever to be a strong mass-based political development. In Women's activist Hypothesis: From Edge to Center, I propose that characterizing woman's rights extensively as "a development to end sexism and chauvinist persecution" would empower us to have a typical political objective… Sharing a shared objective doesn't suggest that ladies and men won't have fundamentally dissimilar viewpoints on how that objective may be reached. (hooks 1989, 23) hooks' methodology relies upon the case that sexism is a specific type of mistreatment that can be recognized from different structures, e.g., prejudice and homophobia, despite the fact that it is presently (and for all intents and purposes generally) interlocked with different types of persecution. Women's liberation's goal is to end sexism, however as a result of its connection to different types of persecution, this will expect endeavors to end different types of mistreatment too. For instance, women's activists who themselves remain bigots can not completely value the expansive effect of sexism on the existences of ladies of variety. Besides on the grounds that misogynist establishments are additionally, e.g., bigot, authoritarian and homophobic, destroying chauvinist foundations will expect that we destroy different types of control entwined with them (Heldke and O'Connor 2004). Taking cues from snares, we could portray woman's rights schematically (permitting the construction to be filled in distinctively by various records) as the view that ladies are dependent upon misogynist abuse and that this is off-base. This move moves the weight of our request from a portrayal of what women's liberation is to a portrayal of what sexism, or chauvinist persecution is.

As referenced above, there are different understandings — women's activist and in any case — of what precisely persecution comprises in, however the main thought is that mistreatment comprises in "an encasing construction of powers and obstructions which keeps an eye on the immobilization and decrease of a gathering or classification of individuals" (Frye 1983, 10-11). In addition to any "encasing structure" is severe, in any case, for conceivably any course of socialization will make a construction that as far as possible and empowers all people who live inside it. On account of mistreatment, in any case, the "encasing structures" being referred to are important for a more extensive framework that unevenly and unreasonably detriments one gathering and advantages another. Thus, e.g., despite the fact that sexism confines the open doors accessible to — thus irrefutably hurts — all kinds of people (and taking into account some pairwise examinations might try and adversely affect a man than a lady), in general, ladies as a gathering unreasonably experience the more noteworthy mischief. It is a pivotal component of contemporary records, notwithstanding, that one can't expect that individuals from the favored gathering have purposefully planned or kept up with the framework for their advantage. The harsh design might be the consequence of an authentic interaction whose originators are a distant memory, or it could be the accidental aftereffect of complicated helpful procedures turned out badly.

Leaving to the side (for the occasion) further subtleties in the record of mistreatment, this has yet to be addressed: What makes a specific type of persecution chauvinist? In the event that we simply say that a type of persecution considers misogynist mistreatment assuming that it hurts ladies, or even fundamentally hurts ladies, this isn't sufficient to recognize it from different types of mistreatment. Basically all types of mistreatment hurt ladies, and apparently some alongside sexism hurt ladies principally (however not only), e.g., body size persecution, age abuse. Additionally, as we've noted previously, sexism isn't simply unsafe to ladies, however is destructive to us all.

What makes a specific type of mistreatment misogynist is by all accounts that it hurts ladies, yet that somebody is dependent upon this type of persecution explicitly in light of the fact that she is (or if nothing else gives off an impression of being) a lady. Racial persecution hurts ladies, yet racial mistreatment (without help from anyone else) doesn't hurt them since they are ladies, it hurts them since they are (or give off an impression of being) individuals from a specific race. The idea that chauvinist mistreatment comprises in persecution to which one is subject by temperance of being or having all the earmarks of being a lady gives us essentially the starting points of a scientific device for recognizing subjecting structures that end up influencing some or even all ladies from those that are all the more explicitly misogynist (Haslanger 2004). Yet, issues and unclarities remain.

To start with, we really want to explain further being persecuted "in light of the fact that you are a lady". E.g., is the possibility that there is a specific type of mistreatment that is well defined for ladies? Is to be persecuted "as a lady" to be mistreated with a certain goal in mind? Or on the other hand might we at any point be pluralists about what chauvinist persecution comprises in without dividing the thought past value?

Two systems for elucidating misogynist mistreatment have shown to be tricky. The first is to keep up with that there is a type of persecution normal to all ladies. For instance, one could decipher Catharine MacKinnon's work as guaranteeing that to be mistreated as a lady is to be seen and treated as physically subordinate, where this guarantee is grounded in the (claimed) widespread truth of the eroticization of male strength and female accommodation (MacKinnon 1987; MacKinnon 1989). In spite of the fact that MacKinnon permits that sexual subjection can occur in a heap of ways, her record is monistic in its endeavor to join the various types of chauvinist persecution around a solitary center record that makes sexual typification the concentration. Despite the fact that MacKinnon's work gives a strong asset to dissecting ladies' subjection, many have contended that it is excessively thin, e.g., in certain unique circumstances (particularly in non-industrial nations) misogynist mistreatment appears to concern more the nearby division of work and financial double-dealing. Albeit positively sexual subjection is a calculate chauvinist mistreatment, it expects us to manufacture doubtful clarifications of public activity to assume that all divisions of work that exploit ladies (as ladies) originate from the "eroticization of predominance and accommodation". Besides, clearly to figure out chauvinist persecution we really want to look for a solitary type of mistreatment normal to all ladies.

A second hazardous methodology has been to consider as ideal models the people who are mistreated exclusively as ladies, with the prospect that perplexing cases getting extra types of persecution will cloud what is particular of chauvinist abuse. This procedure would have us center in the U.S. on White, affluent, youthful, lovely, physically fit, hetero ladies to figure out what persecution, if any, they endure, with the expectation of tracking down sexism in its "most flawless" structure, unmixed with prejudice or homophobia, and so on (see Spelman 1988, 52-54). This approach isn't just imperfect in that frame of mind of everything except the best ladies in its worldview, however it accepts that honor in different regions doesn't influence the peculiarity viable. As Elizabeth Spelman comes to the meaningful conclusion:

…no lady is likely to any type of mistreatment essentially on the grounds that she is a lady; which types of persecution she is likely to rely upon what "kind" of lady she is. In a world in which a lady may be dependent upon bigotry, inequity, homophobia, hostile to Semitism, in the event that she isn't so subject it is a result of her race, class, religion, sexual direction. So it can never be the situation that the treatment of a lady has just to do with her orientation and nothing to do with her group or race. (Spelman 1988, 52-3)

Ongoing records of persecution are intended to permit that abuse takes many structures, and decline to distinguish one structure as more essential or central than the rest. For instance, Iris Youthful portrays five "faces" of mistreatment: abuse, minimization, feebleness, social government, and efficient brutality (Youthful 1990c, Ch. 2). Conceivably others ought to be added to the rundown. Chauvinist or bigoted mistreatment, for instance, will show itself in various ways in various settings, e.g., in certain settings through efficient viciousness, in different settings through financial abuse. Recognizing this doesn't go very sufficiently far, in any case, for monistic scholars, for example, MacKinnon could allow this much. Pluralist records of chauvinist mistreatment should likewise permit that there is definitely not an overall clarification of misogynist persecution that applies to every one of its structures: now and again it is possible that ladies' abuse as ladies is because of the eroticization of male strength, yet in different cases it could be better made sense of by ladies' regenerative worth in laying out connection structures (Rubin 1975), or by the moving requests of globalization inside an ethnically separated working environment. As such, pluralists oppose the impulse to "great social hypothesis," "overall meta narratives," "Mono causal clarifications," to permit that the clarification of sexism in a specific verifiable setting will depend on financial, political, legitimate, and social factors that are well defined for that setting which would keep the record from being summed up to all occurrences of sexism (Fraser and Nicholson 1990). It is as yet viable with pluralist techniques to search out designs in ladies' social positions and underlying clarifications inside and across friendly settings, however in doing so we should be profoundly delicate to verifiable and social variety.

Women's liberation as Against Sexism

Be that as it may, assuming we seek after a pluralist system in understanding misogynist mistreatment, what brings together every one of the examples as occurrences of sexism? All things considered, we can't expect that the mistreatment being referred to takes similar structure in various settings, and we can't accept that there is a fundamental clarification of the various ways it shows itself. So could we at any point try and discuss there being a brought together arrangement of cases — something we can call "misogynist mistreatment" — by any means?

A few women's activists would encourage us to perceive that there is definitely not a methodical method for binding together the various cases of sexism, and correspondingly, there is no deliberate solidarity in what considers woman's rights: rather we ought to see the reason for women's activist solidarity in alliance building (Reagon 1983). Various gatherings work to battle various types of persecution; a few gatherings take mistreatment against ladies (as ladies) as an essential concern. Assuming that there is a reason for participation between some subset of these gatherings in a given setting, then, at that point, observing that premise is an achievement, however ought not be underestimated.

Another option, in any case, is award that by and by solidarity among women's activists can't be underestimated, however regardless a hypothetical shared conviction among women's activist perspectives that doesn't expect that sexism shows up in a similar structure or for similar reasons in all specific situations.We saw over that one promising methodology for recognizing sexism from prejudice, inequity, and different types of treachery is to zero in on the possibility that in the event that an individual is experiencing chauvinist persecution, a significant piece of the clarification why she is dependent upon the shamefulness is that she is or has all the earmarks of being a lady. This remembers cases for which ladies as a gathering are expressly designated by a strategy or a training, yet additionally incorporates situations where the strategy or practice influences ladies because of a background marked by sexism, regardless of whether they are not unequivocally focused on. For instance, on the off chance that ladies are denied a training as are, overall, ignorant. Furthermore, if under these conditions just the people who are educated are qualified for vote. Then, at that point, we can say that ladies as a gathering are being disappointed and that this is a type of chauvinist mistreatment since part of the clarification of why ladies can't cast a ballot is that they are ladies, and ladies are denied a schooling. The shared trait among the cases is to be found in the job of orientation in the clarification of the shamefulness as opposed to the particular structure the foul play takes. Expanding on this we could bind together a wide scope of women's activist perspectives by seeing them as focused on the (exceptionally conceptual) claims that:

(Spellbinding case) Ladies, and the people who seem, by all accounts, to be ladies, are exposed to wrongs or potentially foul play to some extent to some extent since they are or seem, by all accounts, to be ladies.
(Regularizing guarantee) The wrongs/treacheries being referred to in (I) should not to happen and ought to be halted when and where they do.
We have so far been utilizing the term 'mistreatment' freely to cover anything that type of wrong or foul play is at issue. Going on with this purposeful receptiveness in the specific idea of some unacceptable, the inquiry actually remains saying that ladies are

exposed to bad form since they are ladies. To resolve this question, it might assist with thinking about a recognizable uncertainty in the thought "on the grounds that": would we say we are worried here with causal clarifications or defenses? On one hand, the case that somebody is persecuted on the grounds that she is a lady proposes that the best (causal) clarification of the subjection being referred to will make reference to her sex: e.g., Paula is dependent upon misogynist mistreatment at work in light of the fact that the best clarification of why she makes $1.00 less an hour for accomplishing equivalent work as Paul makes reference to her sex (perhaps notwithstanding her race or other social characterizations). Then again, the case that somebody is mistreated on the grounds that she is a lady recommends that the reasoning or reason for the severe designs expects that one be delicate to somebody's sex in deciding how they ought to be seen and treated, i.e., that the legitimization for somebody's being dependent upon the designs being referred to relies upon a portrayal of them as sexed male or female. E.g., Paula is dependent upon misogynist mistreatment at work on the grounds that the compensation scale for her work grouping is legitimate inside a structure that recognizes and debases ladies' work contrasted and men's.

Note, nonetheless, that in the two kinds of cases the way that one is or seems, by all accounts, to be a lady need not be the main element important in making sense of the unfairness. It very well may be, for instance, that one hangs out in a gathering due to one's race, or one's class, or one's sexuality, and on the grounds that one stands apart one turns into an objective for shamefulness. Yet, assuming that the unfairness takes a structure that, e.g., is viewed as particularly able for a lady, then the foul play ought to be perceived diversely, i.e., as a reaction to an interconnected class. For instance, the act of assaulting Bosnian ladies was an interconnected foul play: it designated them both on the grounds that they were Bosnian and on the grounds that they were ladies.

Obviously, these two understandings of being persecuted on the grounds that you are a lady are not contradictory; as a matter of fact they ordinarily support each other. Since human activities are in many cases best made sense of by the structure utilized for legitimizing them, one's sex might assume a huge part in deciding how one is dealt with in light of the fact that the foundation understandings for what's suitable treatment draw harmful differentiation s between the genders. All in all, the causal component for sexism frequently goes through dangerous portrayals of ladies and orientation jobs.

In every one of the instances of being mistreated as a lady referenced above, Paula endures shamefulness, yet a significant consider making sense of the treachery is that Paula is an individual from a specific gathering, viz., ladies (or females). This, we think, is critical in grasping the reason why sexism (and prejudice, and other - isms) are most frequently perceived as sorts of abuse. Abuse is unfairness that, as a matter of some importance, concerns gatherings; people are persecuted in the event they are exposed to bad form due to their gathering enrollment. On this view, to guarantee that ladies as ladies endure shamefulness is to guarantee that ladies are abused.

Where does this leave us? 'Woman's rights' is an umbrella term for a scope of perspectives about treacheries against ladies. There are conflicts among women's activists about the idea of equity overall and the idea of sexism, specifically, the particular sorts of foul play or wrong ladies endure; and the gathering who ought to be the essential focal point of women's activist endeavors. In any case, women's activists are focused on finishing about friendly change up foul play against ladies, specifically, bad form against ladies as ladies.

3. *Points in Women's liberation*: Outline of the Reference book Sub-Passages

Given a schematic system for considering various types of women's liberation, it ought to be more clear the way in which philosophical issues emerge in ironing out the subtleties of a women's activist position. The most clear philosophical responsibility will be to a regulating hypothesis that verbalizes a record of equity as well as a record of the upside. Women's activists have been associated with studying existing regulating speculations and articulating options for quite a while. An overview of a portion of this work can be viewed as under "Women's liberation, mediations", in the sub-passages inside "Women's activist Political Way of thinking", viz., Liberal Woman's rights, Realist Women's liberation, and Revolutionary Women's liberation. (See likewise Hampton 1993; Jaggar 1983; Kittay 1999; MacKinnon 1989; Nussbaum 1999; Okin 1979; Okin 1989; Pateman 1988; Schneir 1972; Schneir 1994; Silvers 1999; Youthful 1990.)

Notwithstanding, there is additionally significant philosophical work to be finished in the thing we have been calling the "graphic" part of woman's rights. Cautious basic consideration regarding our practices can uncover the deficiency of prevailing philosophical figures of speech. For instance, women's activists working according to the viewpoint of ladies' lives have been persuasive in pointing out philosophical the peculiarity of endlessly care giving (Ruddick 1989; Held 1995; Held 2007; Hamington 2006), reliance (Kittay 1999), handicap (Wilkerson 2002; Carlson 2009) ladies' work (Waring 1999; Delphy 1984; Harley 2007), logical predisposition and objectivity (Longino 1990), and have uncovered shortcomings in existing moral, political, and epistemological hypotheses. All the more by and large, women's activists have called for investigation into what are normally thought of "private" practices and individual worries, like the family, sexuality, the body, to adjust what has appeared to be a manly pre-occupation with "public" and generic matters. Reasoning surmises interpretive apparatuses for grasping our regular daily existences; women's activist work in articulating extra components of involvement and parts of our practices is priceless in showing the predisposition in existing devices, and in the quest for better ones.

Women's activist clarifications of sexism and records of chauvinist rehearses likewise raise gives that are inside the space of conventional philosophical request. For instance, in contemplating care, women's activists have posed inquiries about the idea of oneself; in pondering orientation, women's activists have asked what the relationship is between the normal and the social; in pondering sexism in science, women's activists have asked what ought to consider information. In whatever cases standard philosophical records give valuable devices; in different cases, elective recommendations have appeared to be seriously encouraging.

CHAPTER FOUR

The concept of body language in women

In the event that you've have been around ladies you'd be aware, they gab with words as well as with non-verbal communication. Non-verbal communication can offer various hints regarding what they're searching for in you. Also, on the off chance that you sort out the signs, you can sort out ladies.

In any case, most men don't comprehend the unpretentious or unsubtle transfers ownership of she gives through her body, hence passing up the most imperative signs of regardless of whether she loves you, or is in any way shape or form keen on you.

In any case, before that you really want you to visually engage with her-eye contacts are normally the main marker that tells if or not a young lady is into you. The perfect proportion of eye to eye connection is a sign of if or not she is keen on you by any means. On the off chance that it looks positive, you can additionally become somewhat more basic about perusing her non-verbal communication all the more precisely.

Before you begin perusing her non-verbal communication however, look her in the eyes. Assuming she's making a lot of eye to eye connection, that is the primary pointer to see whether she's keen on you by any means. On the off chance that it looks positive, you ought to peruse her non-verbal communication all the more precisely for a few additional positive signs.

Female Non-verbal communication Indications of Fascination

The following are fundamental, yet self-evident, giveaways on how ladies respond through their non-verbal communication assuming that they're keen on you:

She Will Continue To play With Her Hair

At the point when ladies attempt and act coy with you, their hand naturally goes to their hair and they begin spinning it around or quickly move them with their fingers. It either implies she's drawn to you or that she's in the temperament to be a tease around a bit. Anything that it is, ladies playing with their hair, while conversing with you is a decent sign

She'll Streak A Real Grin At You

Assuming you see her grinning really at you, that is areas of strength for another. Assuming her grin is constrained or looks affable, where she's not going on the defensive toward the grin appears to be tight, then, at that point, she's simply being courteous, yet assuming you track down her smiling from one cheek to another, she's most certainly drawn to you, or possibly needs to get to know you.

She'll Nibble Her Lip

Lip gnawing could be an indication of apprehension and on the off chance that you find her doing it while she's conversing with you, you know she's as keen on conversing with you as you are in her. This is an exceptionally subliminal endeavor to stand out, BTW.

Her Body Will Face You

While you're having a discussion with her, perceive how she is standing. Assuming her arms are loose and she's confronting you, that is a positive sign. On the off chance that she's not keen on you, she'll remain in a way that may not be confronting every last bit of her towards you. She will likewise have her arms crossed and have negligible eye to eye connection with you. Those are most certainly signs that she's not intrigued.

She's OK With Contacting

By contact I mean, in the event that she's putting her hand on your shoulders while conversing with you, that is most certainly an indication of her playing with you. In some cases ladies likewise contact themselves accidentally (no, not what you're thinking!), to quiet their fervor. She might rub her thighs or her arms or continue crossing or non-folding her legs either out of fervor or sheer anxiety.

She'll Mirror You

Reflecting is an exceptionally sure sign with non-verbal communication. Reflecting is the point at which she is mimicking your activities subliminally. And that implies, you've started to lead the pack and she's very into you at this point. So assuming that you get your beverage, she'll get hers or on the other hand on the off chance that you fold your legs, she'll cross hers.

Erupting Nostrils

This can't be controlled. She can't do this intentionally and as per specialists in the event that a young lady is drawn towards you, she will erupt her noses. It sounds abnormal yet it is valid as this is wild and assuming this happens simply realize that she loves you.

Different LEG CROSSES

In the event that a lady is folding her legs, possibly she is anxious or this is a demonstration to look for consideration. Additionally, in the event that her knees are pointed towards you, she truly prefers you.

She'll focus on what you are talking about

You'll continuously stand out and regardless of who is tuning in or who isn't she'd constantly be paying attention to anything you're saying. Likewise, she'll uphold the reason or your viewpoints that you're standing firm for.

Dressing

She is constantly fixing herself before you. She could purposely or unconsciously do this as she is gambling with fixing herself before you while she has your consideration as of now since she thinks often about your thought process. Consequently, she is trying to look great and stick out.

In this way, in the event that you've quite recently met her and are uncertain in the event that she loves you or not, simply pay special attention to these unpretentious and unsubtle non-verbal communication signs and you'll have your responses not too far off and afterward! This will simply empower you to be less confounded than you as of now are help you in taking the principal action.

Are Ladies Better Than Men At Perusing Non-verbal communication?

Sorry folks, yet science shows that ladies are better at sending and getting non-verbal communication signs than men. How it's done:

Monica Moore, a teacher of exploratory brain science at Webster College in St. Louis, found men frequently miss a lady's most memorable eye-staring romance sign. By and large, ladies need to eye stare multiple times before a man pays heed.

Ladies may be better at perusing non-verbal communication since a greater amount of their mind is dynamic when they assess others' way of behaving. X-ray filters uncover that ladies have 14 to 16 dynamic mind regions while assessing others, though men just have 4 to 6 dynamic.

Instructions to Tell a Young lady You Like Her

Allow me to take you back to secondary school: You're an off-kilter adolescent kid, and you see your secondary school darling looking straight at you. You don't have the foggiest idea how to ask her out, so everything that's the most effective way to non-verbally say to her you dig her? Would it be a good idea for you:

grin at her

wink at her

show her your muscles

fold around like a chicken

The response?

Confusing question — there is no right response! When you've chosen to flag your advantage, she's probably Currently sent you handfuls — on the off chance that not hundreds — of minuscule miniature signals that demonstrate assuming she's keen on YOU. Signals that could have flown right past you in the event that you don't have the foggiest idea what to search for.

Most early flagging is finished by ladies. Ladies are genuinely the "selectors" who stand out by showing unobtrusive nonverbal signals1. So assuming that you know what to search for, there'd be no requirement for your off-kilter secondary school self to assemble up the boldness to confront dismissal in any case.

So what would it be a good idea for you to search for? This is what to search for to peruse a female's non-verbal communication effectively.

Her Shoulders Will Advance Toward You
Have you at any point had a lady investigate her shoulder or raise it? The shoulders might appear to be honest, however they additionally impersonate the lady's bosom and sexual constitution.

A sideways look over a raised shoulder features bends and the roundness of the female face. This connotes estrogen, uncovered the weakness of the neck, and deliveries pheromones. Ladies naturally do this while attempting to be a tease.
Female non-verbal communication, or the non-verbal communication of ladies, isn't too not the same as that of men. Notwithstanding, female non-verbal communication has a couple of recognizable contrasts that the two genders can make note of. In this extreme aide on female non-verbal communication, I'll show you the 15 prompts that ladies "release" that sign interest, fascination, and, surprisingly, a craving to do somewhat more. □

On the whole…

Her Face Will Show Want

Did you realize ladies' countenances are by and large more expressive than men's? In the event that you give close consideration, a lady who's showing interest signals will spill out indications of want all over.

Assuming that you knew all about the 7 different micro-expressions as of now, you may ponder, "There's no craving articulation, is there?" And you'd be correct! Want isn't one of the 7 all inclusive articulations. In any case, we can really see want in a pulled in lady's face through her lips and eyes:

 Her lips will somewhat part. Are her lips marginally separated? Marginally separated lips additionally copy female genitalia. It proposes the genital "echo."2 Concentrates on demonstrate the way that contacting and stroking the knees can flag sexual interest. Obviously, assuming she's stroking your knee, no requirement for additional inquiries. Be that as it may, assuming that she's stroking hers, this might be a psyche want to stroke yours.

Side Note: You can consider the knees 2 "enormous, leg-molded bolts" that point at an individual's object of interest3. Hope to check whether her knees are highlighting you.

She'll Open Up Her Body

Her non-verbal communication will flag transparency instead of being shut off. Things to search for include:

Arms. Are her arms more open around you? Is it safe to say that they are uninhibitedly moving and not held near her body? Ladies are bound to crease their arms across their middle around forceful or ugly men, yet assuming that they think that you are alluring, they'll open their body up4.

Legs. Crossed legs doesn't be guaranteed to mean she's not into you — this could simply be a fascination signal. Make a point to take note of the course of her knees to check whether she's highlighting you or away from you.

Watch her non-verbal communication, as a more loosened up body shows solace and fascination.

She'll Uncover Her Thigh

Despite the fact that crossing legs might be a shut off signal, a few ladies might fold their legs to uncover their thighs. (Here's a clue: they most certainly know.) Ladies might do this particularly on the off chance that they're wearing a short skirt, shorts, or tight stockings.

↑ List of chapters ↑

She'll Squint More

Dr. David Givens, chief at the Middle for Nonverbal Examinations, says that "quick eye blink (or 'eyelash ripple') implies you've raised the signal's degree of mental excitement." When a lady unexpectedly flickers quicker, you might have expanded her degree of sexual fervor.

You could see an unexpected fast eye flicker when you recount an astonishing story of you being a cool/energizing/interesting person. This is a subconscious approach to saying, "You've caught my advantage."

Here is the squint in real life in an episode of The Lone wolf (timestamp 3:29):

She'll Move Her Hips

How does a lady move, groove, and rotate her hips?

Ladies normally have more extensive hips than men, and a lady who is drawn to you could swing her hips to and fro more than typical. The volatile movement can without much of a stretch be seen while strolling, particularly on the off chance that a lady goes to the bathroom (she'll probably accept at least for now that you're watching).

Search for the hip influence — this development welcomes consideration and misrepresents the totality of her hips and rump.

She'll Stick Her Chest Out

Have you at any point seen a gelada primate? Their chests are really red, flagging sexuality and ripeness.

Not the most alluring mate, yet all the same she's accessible.

Since the bosoms are such a sexual sign, ladies who are drawn to you might adhere their chests out to highlight their bends. You might see her incline nearer, whip her shoulders back, and stand taller to show her products more.

She'll Do the Hair Flip

In the event that you've sat in front of the TV previously (like, ever), you might have seen those Pigeon or Patentee advertisements. The majority of them share one thing for all intents and purpose: stunningly overstated hair flips.

Ladies throw their hair or contact their neck while being a tease since it uncovered the armpit, which deliveries sex chemicals, shows the ebb and flow of the neck, and features gleaming solid hair. Hair flipping is finished to draw attention5. Our eyes are consequently attracted to the hair when a lady flips. It's a nonverbal approach to expressing, "Take a gander at how solid and delightful my hair looks!" Even with extreme lethargies patients, it has been shown they attempt to follow development with their eyes.

Investigate this entertaining Saturday Night Live play where Sofia Vergara and Penelope Cruz sell Pantene cleanser and you'll understand what I mean:

She'll Make Herself Look More Accommodating
Ladies battle with attempting to hold fast while not scaring men. From a non-verbal communication point of view, this occurs in various ways. Ladies use prompts of "accommodation" to show weakness yet can likewise utilize specific moves for confidence, to show they are not weaklings.

Ladies pluck their eyebrows higher up their temple since it makes them look more powerless. This causes a chemical delivery in a man's mind associated with securing and guarding the female.

Strangely, a limp wrist or uncovered wrists are an indication of accommodation, and the two ladies and gay men will generally subliminally do this when in a room with individuals they need to draw in. Very much like how feeble prey in the wild could take off from its hunters, a limp wrist welcomes one more to overwhelm her. This is the reason while smoking, numerous ladies hold the cigarette with one wrist ended up and uncovered.

At the point when ladies need to be self-assured, they can remain with their feet spread farther separated. This "guaranteeing of an area" is an inner mind prompt to men that the lady is feeling sure.

She'll Make the Marilyn Monroe Face
Like Marilyn Monroe, ladies who are attempting to tempt a man will more often than not cause a commotion and lower their covers since it seems to be like the face ladies make when they are encountering joy.

She'll Dress Herself
Ladies will continually dress themselves to amplify their appeal. At the point when around a man she enjoys, trimming ways of behaving may go up1:

Ladies stroke their hair and spin it around their fingers. They could try and do this unknowingly while conversing with somebody they like. Dressing the hair causes it to look more appealing prepped, however it additionally causes to notice the hair since our eyes are drawn to development.

A few ladies might put on cosmetics, in any event, during a date. On the off chance that she pardons herself to the restroom, and you notice a new layer of lipstick, this is a sign she's attempting to put her best self forward. Give close consideration to her appearance when she goes to the bathroom — you could see little however unpretentious changes!

Looking in the mirror. In the event that you're strolling by a mirror or window, you could see her giving close consideration to her appearance. She may be checking to ensure she puts her best self forward.

She'll Gradually Touch Close by Items

In the event that the longing to contact is areas of strength for so, it could be improper to do as such, you could see her conduct move to contacting different articles:

A lady might touch, stroke, and caress a wine glass or the cup she's drinking from. This is a type of item transaction. Objects that are phallic in nature might try and become possibly the most important factor, like a pen or even her telephone.

Squirming with keys is one more type of item transaction. She could stroke her vehicle keys or rub them between her fingers to deliver her repressed energy.

Female Non-verbal communication Ways to be a tease

Considering a portion of the female non-verbal communication signals, here are a few hints for all kinds of people to be a non-verbal communication love master:

While moving toward a lady, men ought to never come up from behind, as this will put her careful. They are in an ideal situation coming in at a point and afterward remaining at a point.

You don't have to have ideal hopes to draw in a man. Concentrates on show that men are more drawn to an in lady tease conduct to show she is accessible, versus the most attractive lady in the room.

What really do individuals consider "affable" non-verbal communication? Here are a portion of the ways of behaving that are alluring and agreeable across friendly, business, and heartfelt circumstances:

grinning

having an expressive face

keeping your hands underneath jawline level (above should be visible as forceful or overanimated)

negligible arm crossing

keeping hands beyond pockets

triple head gestures to show interest

private eye staring (from the eyes to the mouth to the body)

inclining in the direction of the other individual

unobtrusive reflecting

THE Study OF Non-verbal communication

Understanding and perusing female non-verbal communication can assist men with understanding ladies better. For instance, numerous men concentrate on female non-verbal communication for of deciding when ladies are drawn to them. They search for female non-verbal communication signals to sort out the thing ladies are thinking. Men in hetero connections might concentrate on female non-verbal communication to more readily decipher the mind-sets and perspectives of their accomplices or mates.

We should investigate what non-verbal communication really implies, what's the significance here to be a lady, and afterward the way that ladies pass their feelings and perspectives on through their non-verbal communication signals. Remember that there are no immovable standards with regards to perusing female non-verbal communication, or perusing non-verbal communication for anybody. What female non-verbal communication and looks mean to one individual could mean another thing to another, including the specialists or clinical analyst. Indeed, even the individual displaying the non-verbal communication could have an alternate understanding of why they're standing or utilizing their arms a specific way. Eventually, the main individual who can decipher their body developments is the individual displaying that non-verbal communication in any case.

By definition, non-verbal communication can incorporate any reflexive or non-reflexive development or token of all or part of the body. The investigation of perusing both female and male non-verbal communication is called kinesics. This is a generally understudied area of brain science, in spite of the fact that a lot more examinations are being finished to characterize and look at non-verbal communication across societies and valuable encounters. Clinical investigations, similar to those completed at Webster College, have shown that non-verbal communication in some cases goes against verbal messages, making it a significant review for individuals, particularly however who utilize open non-verbal communication as a decent indication of fascination.

A significant part of the study of non-verbal communication for those intrigued is that it influences across world societies. You need to peruse non-verbal communication in its social setting. The non-verbal communication we notice in individuals in certain pieces of Europe, for instance, may contrast significantly from non-verbal communication displayed by ladies in the U.S. For this article, the non-verbal communication of most ladies in the U.S. is recorded by models.

Specialists concur that while words are utilized as essential correspondence, non-verbal communication improves at of conveying mentality and feeling. At times, non-verbal communication might sub for verbal correspondence. Along these lines, it is essential to have the option to decipher the non-verbal communication and nonverbal correspondence of the ladies in your day to day existence precisely, particularly assuming that you are attempting to decide profound fascination or even old flame.

Non-verbal communication Of Ladies

The non-verbal communication of ladies in the U.S. is genuinely standard and depends on hundreds of years of social predispositions and assumptions for ladies. Numerous ladies want to be amenable and maybe even docile in their verbal correspondences because of the spot that ladies have customarily held in the public eye. This is valid in the vast majority of their social cooperations, from the expert circle to a first date or even a discussion with a male companion. Be that as it may, their non-verbal communication will frequently tell the story of how they are feeling, regardless of whether they end up feeling something contrary to what they're communicating with their words.

Head Slants

The slant of the head can show individuals that you are paying attention to them or empowering them to talk. It shows that the audience needs to flag interest in the inquiry or answer being introduced to them. Numerous ladies slant their heads while having discussions with individuals, particularly in discussions with individuals who they feel hold authority over them.

A head slant can likewise be perused as an indication of accommodation. Numerous men see a lady shifting her head as a sign that she expects that the men are in places of control. The lady may not intend to convey this, yet it is much of the time how men in power read that sign. For ladies, if you need to radiate fearlessness and authority, keep your head straight while conversing with a man who you see to be in a place of control. Somebody ladies will shift their head frequently with a twofold or triple head slant, yet certainty and authority frequently comes from a straight head.

Level And Space

The level and space that an individual takes up can show a great deal about their mentality and feelings. Numerous ladies consolidate themselves to occupy as little room as could be expected. This is a type of female non-verbal communication that has been gone down through ages, as ladies have been accommodating to men and ordinarily not in, influential places. This conduct is an immediate consequence of the social assumptions that ladies hold. A lady consolidating herself into a little space or having a slumping stance shows that she is compliant and not in charge.

Then again, a lady who is sitting or standing exceptionally straight, shoulders back, and feet spread separated shows a demeanor of telling and authority. At the point when a lady is utilizing this non-verbal communication, it shows that a lady feels she is in charge of the circumstance and she is requesting regard. She'll believe that individuals should focus closer on them, and she extends the actual presence of her body by putting her arms out, keeping her legs tall and straight, holding her head high, and showing a general quality of control with areas of strength for a.

Assuaging Signals

Signals during talking or paying attention to other people, like playing with hair or adornments, snatching upper arms, or contacting the neck can frequently imply that the lady is anxious or pushed. A man could attempt to add something extra to ladies whirling their hair or scouring their shoulders, and he'll make an off-base presumption that she's drawn to him. Certain individuals professing to be specialists let men know that playing with hair or gems or contacting the neck is an indication that the lady is drawn to you.

Truly, actual touch or squirming of hair or gems is an indication of misery. It can show that ladies need more space, or that they are anxious in the ongoing circumstance. As a man, it is critical to have the option to peruse this non-verbal communication of individuals for what it is and make her more OK with the discussion or end the discussion completely on the off chance that she is apprehensively tinkering with something like her hair or gems.

Grinning

A great many people expect that when somebody grins it is an indication of cordiality and satisfaction. In any case, what many individuals don't understand is that numerous ladies grin (or if nothing else bend their lips upwards) when they are anxious like when they display dressing ways of behaving. This implies that a few ladies might grin exorbitantly or at improper times, making their feelings and nonverbal signals hard to peruse. A grin isn't as clear an indication of interest as most men suspect.

Generally speaking, it is vital to truly pay attention to the expressions of the lady you are conversing with as opposed to simply focusing on her grin. Give close consideration: watch, tune in, and decide whether the grin is certified or just put on. Search for other non-verbal communication signals that could tell you that she is bothered instead of blissful and agreeable. Apprehension will as a rule show itself in alternate ways as examined above like playing with hair.

Gesturing

Numerous ladies gesture significantly more oftentimes than men. There are kids about ladies seeming like bobble-sets out toward this explanation. At the point when a man gestures, it normally implies that he concurs with what is being said. This could be valid for a lady too, albeit a head gesture could likewise imply that she is tuning in or empowering you to talk.

As a lady, it is essential to know about gesturing. Men frequently don't comprehend that a gesture can amount to something other than understanding or accommodation. Assuming you gesture too often, your non-verbal communication can be effectively misread, and men could ask why you concur with them when in all actuality you are simply listening eagerly to what they need to say.

At the point when you see a lady gesturing her head when you converse with her, consciously inquire as to whether she's concurring with you or tuning in and grasping you. At the point when you gesture when a lady is talking with you, tell her that you concur with what she's talking about.

Inclining Forward

Numerous ladies incline forward when they are associated with an extreme discussion. In any case, this can frequently be confounded as a way for the lady to cause to notice herself. In any case, that is not their motivation to incline forward. Ladies likewise incline forward when they are coquettish, and this is in many cases how men decipher this female non-verbal communication.

Men should peruse this non-verbal communication in setting with the present circumstance and the discussion. Assuming that in an expert climate and a warmed or extraordinary discussion, all things considered, the lady is just extremely connected as opposed to effectively being a tease. Simultaneously, ladies should know about this inclination and how flagging interest might be deciphered.

Genuinely Expressive Hand Signals

Numerous ladies "talk with their hands," implying that when they get genuinely put resources into a discussion, they utilize expressive hand signals. It's actual in circumstances with their companions, accomplice, or even in proficient settings. This can make the presence of being sincerely put resources into the ongoing discussion. Utilizing a ton of sincerely expressive hand signals can pass on to the next individual that the lady is excessively genuinely involved or put resources into the subject of the discussion. Thusly, we see these non-verbal communication signs with men. At the point when men areexcessively close to home, they will normally puff out their chests, develop their voices, and increment the volume of their voices.

Ladies must comprehend that excessively expressive hand motions in the U.S., especially those at or over the shoulders, are generally perused as a sign that the lady isn't in charge of herself or her feelings. If a lady has any desire to be treated in a serious way or found in a, strategic, influential place in a work environment that is for the most part comprised of men, any hand signals ought to be negligible and kept at or underneath the midriff.

Handshake Strength

How a lady shakes your hand can say a ton regarding the lady. A feeble handshake can pass on to the beneficiary that the lady is compliant, bashful, threatened, apprehensive, or the entirety of the above mentioned. In another circumstance, a solid handshake tells the beneficiary that the lady is sure and in a, influential place and control. It can likewise address areas of strength for her and common sense.

Eye Rolling

Numerous ladies are inclined to visit eye rolling. Moving the eyes is typically an indication of restlessness or dissatisfaction. At the point when you see a lady feigning exacerbation, however being verbally tranquil or saved, this could be an indication of her attempting to stay courteous yet becoming annoyed. It is critical to peruse this sign for what it is and change your strategy with the discussion or end the discussion totally.

Eye to eye connection

Direct eye to eye connection, or the absence of some, can be perused in different ways. At the point when ladies hold direct eye to eye connection, they are normally completely participated in the discussion and are not being compliant at all. They might be visually connecting to tell you that they are focusing on you. A few men read direct eye to eye connection as an indication of fascination, however this isn't generally the situation.

Simultaneously, an absence of direct eye to eye connection in a lady may be perused as an indication of accommodation. At the point when a lady sees you then peers down, it tends to be viewed as coy yet additionally a token of being accommodating to the man she is conversing with. Absence of eye to eye connection can likewise be an indication that she's remaining quiet about something. An adjustment of the understudy size during eye to eye connection can convey a similar importance.

Assuming you're passing a lady in the lobby at work, for instance, and she doesn't look at you straightforwardly in the eye after you express welcome to her, that could imply that she's telling you she's not keen on you. Your expectation probably won't have been to convey this sort of interest, yet she doesn't have a clue about that. She could try not to take a gander at you straightforwardly, for dread on the off chance that she did, you could confound this way of behaving as interest. On the off chance that she looked at you without flinching however, you could move toward her with the desire for getting to know her better or in any event, asking her out. Once more, this could have been the farthest thing from your psyche, yet once more, she doesn't have a clue about that. As opposed to face the challenge of dismissing somebody who might actually and perhaps perilously fight back against her, she stays away from this present circumstance by and large by not checking out at you straightforwardly in any case.

Crossing Arms

At the point when a lady folds her arms (or her legs while she's sitting), it can cause to notice one of a few things. Many individuals fold their arms when they are feeling guarded, for example, during a contention or in a circumstance where they feel undermined. Ladies likewise fold their arms to communicate conflict with somebody during a discussion or contention. A few ladies likewise fold their arms when they are exhausted with the discussion and are prepared for it to end. Also, a few ladies, or individuals as a rule, fold their arms when they feel cold. It is vital to consider the words she says when you read non-verbal communication that the lady is utilizing to accurately decipher this message.

Tapping Or Drumming Fingers

The tapping or drumming of fingers on a table or other surface is typically an indication of fretfulness or fatigue. The one who drums her fingers on the table is burnt out on the discussion or circumstance that she is in. She might be worn out on pausing, or she might be becoming disappointed with an uneven discussion. One more justification for tapping or drumming fingers is the point at which a lady is pondering something or going to go with a choice. Thus, assuming that you see her tapping her wine glass, it very well may be an ideal opportunity to drop or change the discussion, or to let her think.

Open Palm Or Uncovered Wrist

A few ladies could uncover a wrist or show an open palm when they feel compliant, frequently without understanding that they are doing as such. They do it without a cognizant contribution from their mind. An uncovered wrist or palm may be an indication that the lady is prepared to do as you request from her, and that implies she is bowing to your position. One more justification behind the uncovered wrist or palm is that she is available to ideas of what you might want to do or say straightaway.

Ladies should perceive these kinds of motions, so they can know about what others could confuse as accommodation or indications of friendship. In any case, in the event that a lady feels compliant, she can change her position by directing her feet to the individual she is tuning in or conversing with and keep her head straight and her hands close by. On the off chance that a lady is available to ideas, alongside this motion, she can express that she's available to ideas. However, this won't be guaranteed to mean she'll concur with those ideas.

By and large, an open palm or palms can have differing implications. Seeing anybody with an open palm(s) could then be perused in more than one way. This is one explanation perusing non-verbal communication can be a test to learn and do.

Locked Lower legs

At the point when a lady locks her lower legs either while sitting or while standing it tends to be an indication that she is anxious or bothered by the discussion. On the off chance that a lady is available to a discussion from the get go in any case, she'll lock her legs at the lower legs as she keeps on sitting, it very well may be a sign that the discussion has entered a spot or subject with which she isn't happy. In any case, this isn't really valid for all ladies, as certain ladies fold their legs at the lower leg normally.

A few ladies were likewise instructed that on the off chance that wearing a dress and sitting, they ought to lock their lower legs. The thought behind this motion is to show individuals that the lady is a woman. Luckily, this chauvinist thought of a lady being a "woman" and show "genteel ways of behaving" is being consigned to the garbage pile.

Expanded Eyes

Research has demonstrated that the eyes expand when the singular sees something that they need. This is valid for ladies similarly however much it is valid for men. Assuming you are conversing with a lady in a group environment and her eyes expand when you ask her for a date, she is telling you without even a second's pause that she is keen on going out with you. In the event that you present a lady with a choice that she's keen on, for example, an advancement or a sought after project, you will likewise get this reaction.

Quickly Flickering Eyes

A few men imagine that flickering eyes are an indication that a lady is drawn to them. They consider this to be a strategy off being a tease. Nonetheless, this is most often not the situation. Most frequently, ladies quickly squint their eyes when they are apprehensive or awkward here and there. In the event that you approach a lady and her eyes are quickly squinting, it is an indication that she is restless and potentially feeling undermined.

Lip Motions

Ladies frequently chomp their lips, including their lower lip when they are worried, stressed, or restless. Be that as it may, numerous men inaccurately perceive gnawing lips to mean fascination and want. Most frequently, in the event that gnawing lips is intended to address want, it will be joined by extraordinary eye to eye connection. If not, a non-verbal communication master could advise you to accept gnawing lips as a sign that she is apprehensive or focused.

One lip motion that can constantly be deciphered accurately is the fixing or tightening of the lips. At the point when a lady fixes her lips, it implies that she'll feel objecting or doubting of the individual she is conversing with. In the event that you approach a lady socially and she'll fixes her lips when you attempt to converse with her, leave the work and continue on.

Hands On Hips

Numerous men can connect with seeing a lady put her hands on her hips during a contention or when a contention is going to be sent off. Putting hands on hips is generally seen by men as a demonstration of hostility with respect to most ladies. Hands on hips can likewise imply that the lady feels she is in charge of the circumstance, which can draw consideration.

What Are The Indications Of A Lady Being a tease?

Perusing female non-verbal communication in this setting can be challenging to peruse, as only one out of every odd lady will act or respond something similar. Many indications of a lady showing that she's drawn in or keen on you incorporate that she'll grin with more than her lips and show actual touch, solid eye to eye connection, and giggling. Nonetheless, as expressed prior, signs like grinning could demonstrate anxiety, so make certain to focus on different signs as well as to try not to make presumptions about any fascination or future expected relationship.

What Are Indications Of Fascination?

A considerable lot of similar marks of fascination are divided among people, however one indication of fascination is giggling. As per speed dating test held in 2018, not entirely settled to be a potential sign of fascination. Different indications of fascination can likewise incorporate eye to eye connection batting of the eyes and grinning. Actual touch can likewise be a sign of sexual interest. Assuming she's drawn to you, she'll stroke your arm or do something that causes to notice her own actual fascination as you are collaborating. Delayed and reliable eye to eye connection is one more mark of close consideration and conceivable fascination.

How Might You Let Know if A Young lady Preferences You Through Non-verbal communication?

Non-verbal communication that could be an indication that a lady is intrigued frequently areas of strength for incorporate contact during discussion and exhibiting that she's agreeable around you. This can be displayed in her casual stance, where her arms probably won't be crossed and she is dynamic in the discussion you are having. One more extraordinary indication of sexual fervor is the point at which she'll lick her lips. Licking lips is something inconspicuous, however it causes to notice her physically alluring highlights, and to make you ponder kissing her. Nonetheless, it could likewise imply that she has a dry mouth and lips, so don't add a lot to this sign.

One more clear sign that she is drawn to you is that she will likewise reasonable grin and chuckle all through the discussion, showing that she is locked in and keen on what you need to say. Assuming she grins really and keeps in touch all through the discussion, it's an extraordinary sign that she could be keen on you sincerely.

Finding support With Correspondence

Assuming you observe that you are as often as possible perusing your accomplice inaccurately, you should get some extra assistance with correspondence. A face to face or online specialist can assist you with figuring out how to (for the most part) accurately decipher female non-verbal communication and looks, and show you how to have more open and productive discussions with your accomplice or mate. In the event that you're a lady, you should investigate assuming that you feel compliant in specific circumstances and how to collect more trust in your non-verbal communication and looks, so you're not sending an agreeable message to other people. This can be particularly advantageous in private and work connections for those intrigued.

Whether you need to figure out how to answer ladies better or you're a lady who needs to radiate more certainty to the rest of the world, online treatment has been demonstrated to be similarly essentially as successful as eye to eye treatment. In an investigation of 26 members getting on the web and in-person mental conduct treatment (changing pessimistic contemplation s and ways of behaving) to treat side effects of uneasiness, stress, and bad quality of life, results showed that web-based treatment was equivalent to conventional treatment. Online mental conduct treatment was additionally displayed to decrease misery side effects fundamentally.

CONCLUSION

In all parts of the vocation, from the receipt of the Ph.D. to passage into the workforce to achieving the position of full teacher, ladies are a rising presence, both in outright number and as an extent of all researchers and designers. However sure and empowering as these progressions may be, it is similarly evident that significant contrasts remain. Ladies as a gathering stay less very much addressed and less fruitful than men in each element of the vocation that we have analyzed. For instance, ladies stay under 50% of new Ph.D.s, are relatively less inclined to enter the full-time logical and designing workforce, are less inclined to stand firm on further developed footholds in industry or the scholarly community, and get lower compensations even in the wake of adapting to contrasts in age, field, and kind of work.

In trying to comprehend the reason why ladies are less all around addressed and less fruitful than men, we worked to abstain from making decisions with respect to the inspirations of those deciding the result of the logical profession, both of the researcher herself as she travels through the existence course, or of the guardians and foundations that control the vocations of youthful

Public Institutes of Sciences, Designing, and Medication. 2001. From Shortage to Perceivability: Distinctions in sexual orientation in the Vocations of Doctoral Researchers and Specialists.

BIBLIOGRAPHY

- WHO. Celebrate International Day of the Midwife [Internet]. 2015 [cited 2017 Sep 7]. p. 1. Available from: http://www.who.int/maternal_child_adolescent/news_events/events/2015/international-day-midwife/en/

- Sandburg C. Being Born is Important. In: Breathing Tokens. Houghton-Mifflin Harcourt; 1978. p. 192.

- Bolt B. Art beyond representation: The performative power of the image. London: I.B. Tauris and Co. Ltd; 2004. 256 p.

- Burton N, editor. Natal signs: Cultural representations of pregnancy, birth and parenting. Bradford: Demeter Press; 2015. 378 p.

- Smithsonian Institution. What does it mean to be human?: Art & music [Internet]. 2017 [cited 2017 May 8]. Available from: http://humanorigins.si.edu/evidence/behavior/art-music

- Encyclopedia of Art Education. History of Art [Internet]. Visual Arts Encyclopedia. 2017 [cited 2017 May 8]. Available from: http://www.visual-arts-cork.com/index.htm

- O'Bannon G. A book review of The Birth Symbol by Max Cameron. Orient Rug Rev. 1983;11(2).

- Musacchio J. The Art and Ritual of Childbirth in Renaissance Italy. New Haven: Yale University Press; 1999. 228 p.

- Beger D, Beaman M. Childbirth education curriculum: An analysis of parent and educator choices. *Journal of Perinatal Education.* 1996;5(4):29–35. [Google Scholar]

- Bergum V. 1989. Woman to mother: A transformation. Granby, MA: Bergin & Garvey. [Google Scholar]

- Bradley R. A. 1965. Husband-coached childbirth. New York: Harper & Row. [Google Scholar]

- Dick-Read G. 1944. Childbirth without fear: The principles and practice of natural childbirth. New York: Harper & Brothers. [Google Scholar]

- Enkin M, Keirse M, Renfrew M, Neilson J. 1999. A guide to effective care in pregnancy & childbirth (2nd ed. Oxford, UK: Oxford University Press. [Google Scholar]

- Fleury J. D. The index of readiness: Development and psychometric analysis. *Journal of Nursing Measurement.* 1994;2:143–154. [PubMed] [Google Scholar]

- Gagnon A. J. 2004. Individual or group antenatal education for childbirth/parenthood. In The Cochrane Library (Vol. Issue 4.

Chichester, UK: John Wiley & Sons. [PubMed] [Google Scholar]

- Glaser B. G. 1978. Theoretical sensitivity: Advances in the methodology of grounded theory. Mill Valley, CA: Sociology Press. [Google Scholar]

- Glaser B. G. 1992. Basics of grounded theory analysis. Mill Valley, CA: Sociology Press. [Google Scholar]

- Glaser B. G, Strauss A. L. 1967. The discovery of grounded theory: Strategies for qualitative research. New York: Aldine De Gruyter. [Google Scholar]

- Green J. M, Baston H. A. Feeling in control during labor: Concepts, correlates, and consequences. *Birth*. 2003;30:235–247. [PubMed] [Google Scholar]

- Hallgren A, Kihlgren M, Norberg A, Forslin L. Women's perceptions of childbirth and childbirth education before and after education and birth. *Midwifery*. 1995;11:130–137. [PubMed] [Google Scholar]

- Humenick S. S. 2000. Program evaluation. In F. H. Nichols & S. S. Humenick (Eds.), Childbirth education: Practice, research, & theory (2nd ed., pp. 593–608. Philadelphia: W.B. Saunders. [Google Scholar]

- Jones L. C. 1983. A meta-analytic study of the effects of childbirth education research from 1960 to 1981. Unpublished doctoral dissertation, Texas A&M. [Google Scholar]

- Koehn M. L. Effectiveness of prepared childbirth and childbirth satisfaction. *Journal of Perinatal Education.* 1992;1(2):35–43. [Google Scholar]

- Koehn M. L. Childbirth education outcomes: An integrative review of the literature. *Journal of Perinatal Education.* 2002;11(3):10–19. [PMC free article] [PubMed] [Google Scholar]

- Lamaze F. 1970. Painless childbirth: Psychoprophylactic method (L. R. Celestin, Trans. Chicago: Henry Regnery. [Google Scholar]

- Lederman R. P. 1996. Psychosocial adaptation in pregnancy: Assessment of seven dimensions of maternal development (2nd ed. New York: Springer. [Google Scholar]

- Lincoln Y. S, Guba E. G. Establishing trustworthiness. 1985. In Naturalistic inquiry (pp. 289–331). Beverly Hills, CA: Sage.

- Malnory M. E. Developmental care of the pregnant couple. *Journal of Obstetric, Gynecologic, and Neonatal Nursing.* 1996;25:525–532. [PubMed] [Google Scholar]

- Martell L. K. From innovation to common practice: Perinatal nursing pre-1970 to 2005. *Journal of Perinatal and Neonatal Nursing.* 2006;20:8–16. [PubMed] [Google Scholar]

- Meleis A. L, Sawyer L. M, Eun-Ok I, Messias D. K. H, Schumacher K. Experiencing transitions: An emerging middle-range theory. *Advances in Nursing Science.* 2000;23:12–28. [PubMed] [Google Scholar]

- Mercer R. T. 1995. Becoming a mother. New York: Springer. [Google Scholar]

- Mercer R. T. Becoming a mother versus maternal role attainment. *Journal of Nursing Scholarship.* 2004;36:226–232. [PubMed] [Google Scholar]

- Nichols F. H. The meaning of the childbirth experience: A review of the literature. *Journal of Perinatal Education.* 1996;5(4):71–77. [Google Scholar]

- Nichols F. H, Gennaro S. 2000. The childbirth experience. In F. H. Nichols & S. S. Humenick (Eds.), Childbirth education: Practice, research, and theory (2nd ed., pp. 66–83. Philadelphia: W.B. Saunders. [Google Scholar]

- Nolan M. Antenatal education—Where next? *Journal of Advanced Nursing.* 1997;25:1198–1204. [PubMed] [Google Scholar]

- Nolan M. Antenatal education: Past and future agendas. *The Practising Midwife.* 1999;2(3):24–27. [PubMed] [Google Scholar]

- Qualitative Solutions and Research Pty. Ltd. QSR NUD*IST (Version 4. 1997. Thousand Oaks, CA: Scolari.

- Rubin R. 1984. Maternal identity and the maternal experience. New York: Springer. [Google Scholar]

- Sims-Jones N, Graham S, Crowe K, Nigro S, McLean B. Prenatal class evaluation. *International Journal of Childbirth Education.* 1998;13(3):28–32. [Google Scholar]

- Slaninka S. C, Galbraith A. M, Strzelecki S, Cockroft M. Collaborative research project. *Journal of Perinatal Education.* 1996;5(3):29–36. [Google Scholar]

- Spiby H, Slade P, Escott D, Henderson B, Fraser R. B. Selected coping strategies in labor: An investigation of women's experiences. *Birth.* 2003;30:189–194. [PubMed] [Google Scholar]

- Stamler L. L. The participants' views of childbirth education: Is there congruency with an enablement framework for education? *Journal of Advanced Nursing.* 1998;28:939–947. [PubMed] [Google Scholar]

- Sullivan P. Felt learning needs of pregnant women. *The Canadian Nurse.* 1993;89(1):42–45. [PubMed] [Google Scholar]

- U.S. Department of Health and Human Services. 2000. Healthy people 2010: Understanding and improving health (2nd ed. Washington, DC: U.S. Government Printing Office. Retrieved November 14, 2007, from http://www.healthypeople.gov/Document/tableofcontents.htm#under. [Google Scholar]

- Alexander, M. Jacqui and Lisa Albrecht, eds. 1998. The Third Wave: Feminist Perspectives on Racism, New York: Kitchen Table: Women of Color Press.

- Anderson, Elizabeth. 1999. "What is the Point of Equality?" Ethics, 109(2): 287-337.

- Anzaldúa, Gloria, ed. 1990. Making Face, Making Soul: Haciendo Caras, San Francisco: Aunt Lute Books.

- Baier, Annette C. 1994. Moral Prejudices: Essays on Ethics, Cambridge, MA: Harvard University Press.

- Barker, Drucilla and Edith Kuiper. 2010 Feminist Economics, New York: Routledge.

- Barrett, Michèle. 1991. The Politics of Truth: From Marx to Foucault, Stanford, CA: Stanford University Press.

- Bartky, Sandra. 1990. "Foucault, Femininity, and the Modernization of Patriarchal Power." In her Femininity and Domination, New York: Routledge, 63-82.

- Basu, Amrita. 1995. The Challenge of Local Feminisms: Women's Movements in Global Perspective, Boulder, CO: Westview Press.

- Baumgardner, Jennifer and Amy Richards. 2000. Manifesta: Young Women, Feminism, and the Future, New York: Farrar, Straus, and Giroux.

- Beauvoir, Simone de. 1974 (1952). The Second Sex, Trans. and Ed. H. M. Parshley. New York: Vintage Books.

- Benhabib, Seyla. 1992. Situating the Self: Gender, Community, and Postmodernism in Contemporary Ethics, New York: Routledge.

- Bergmann, Barbara. 2002. The Economic Emergence of Women (Second edition) New York: Palgrave, St. Martin's Press.

- Breines, Wini. 2002. "What's Love Got to Do with It? White Women, Black Women, and Feminism in the Movement Years," Signs: Journal of Women in Culture and Society, 27(4): 1-095-1133.

- Brownmiller, Susan. 1975. Against Our Will: Men, Women, and Rape, New York: Bantam.

- Calhoun, Cheshire. 2000. Feminism, the Family, and the Politics of the Closet: Lesbian and Gay Displacement, Oxford: Oxford University Press.

- ——. 1989. "Responsibility and Reproach." Ethics, 99(2): 389-406.
- Campbell, Sue, hetitia Meynell and Susan Sherwin. 2009. Embodiment and Agency, University Park, PA: Penn State Press.
- Carlson, Licia. 2009. The Faces of Intellectual Disability: Philosophical Reflections, Bloomington, IN: Indiana University Press.
- Collins, Patricia Hill. 1990. Black Feminist Thought, Boston, MA: Unwin Hyman.
- Cott, Nancy. 1987. The Grounding of Modern Feminism, New Haven: Yale University Press.